Jack
in
Pemberland

HERSCHEL HARDIN

◆ FriesenPress

One Printers Way
Altona, MB R0G 0B0
Canada

www.friesenpress.com

Copyright © 2024 by Herschel Hardin
First Edition — 2024

All rights reserved.

No part of this publication may be reproduced in any form, or by any means, electronic or mechanical, including photocopying, recording, or any information browsing, storage, or retrieval system, without permission in writing from FriesenPress.

ISBN
978-1-03-830905-1 (Hardcover)
978-1-03-830904-4 (Paperback)
978-1-03-830906-8 (eBook)

1. FICTION, POLITICAL

Distributed to the trade by The Ingram Book Company

BY THE SAME AUTHOR

Non-fiction
A Nation Unaware: The Canadian Economic Culture
Closed Circuits: The Sellout of Canadian Television
The Privatization Putsch
The New Bureaucracy: Waste and Folly in the Private Sector
Working Dollars: The VanCity Story

Plays
Esker Mike and his Wife, Agiluk
The Great Wave of Civilization
The New World Order

To Marguerite

1
Jack and Billy

I was strolling down The Drive one Saturday morning, enjoying the ambiance of it while I could – everything in Vancouver is changing so quickly, becoming gentrified, bourgeoisified, concretified, who knows if it will be around tomorrow? – then who should I run into but an old rugger acquaintance of mine, Jack Lewicki. He looked at me stunned, which was unusual for him, such an outgoing guy, but despite his awkward body language, he seemed to be glad to see me.

It was his staring at me, as if calculating, that caught my attention.

"Boy, am I happy to run across you," he said, finally, and gave me a full-body hug.

"What the hell?" I thought. "What's this all about? I haven't seen him for years, and now he's hugging me." All of which made me doubly curious.

Even if we had lost touch, Jack and I went back a long way, to our rugby days. If you drink enough beer and swap enough dirty jokes with somebody in the crowd, you're not likely to forget him. Jack and I, though, had an even more personal connection: He fractured my skull. You read that correctly, that's exactly what he did. We were serious rugby players. I was a centre and fast off the mark with the ball, if I say so myself. When I saw a gap in the defensive line, that particular game, I went for it. Instead of passing the ball I cut back in with gusto, head down, and then, bam! I went out like a stone. Jack, on the other team, had hit me high, caught by my sudden change of direction.

We had nicknames for each other. Jack was Jackass Lewicki. I, Billy McIntyre – I've never been called Bill, much less William – was Billy Goat McIntyre. Billy Goat, the rugby god said at that moment, meet Jackass, which is what happened.

They imprisoned me in hospital for a day or so, waking me up occasionally while I rested, and decorated my skull with a full-head plaster cast which made me look like a swami. Being a wannabe tough guy, I went to work on the third day after, groggy as I was. I was at our homestead, aka the boutique law firm McIntyre, McIntyre (my brother, Elvis), Dhaliwal, and Rosen, when who should walk in the door that very morning, unannounced, but Jack himself.

He looked at me and roared with laughter.

"Why don't you look where you're going?" he exclaimed, hardly containing himself.

By the time we had finished making up, he had convinced me to let him autograph my skull, which he did – only at the back, though, I have my limits – with a felt pen. "With fondest regards, Jack," he wrote. Who said rugby players don't have a non-porn sense of humour?

I knew, though, there was something heartfelt behind his gesture, not least because he would have needed to take a day off work to drop by.

What else did I know about him? Well, he was as macho as they come. And, befitting his temperament, he drove a concrete truck. He used to regale us with stories of being king of the roost, up in the cab, with 30 odd tons of weight behind him, "leaving his droppings," as he put it, his own mark and signature, in every new foundation and rebar wall worth their name in the city. Like a father who had given birth to this building and that, he could point them out as he walked around downtown from one bar to another, making aspersive comments about this developer and that architect as he went along, with adulterous affairs attached if any, like the chronicler of a rogue's gallery. He seemed to know everyone, and everyone's secrets.

This day, though, years later, he had changed, in subtle ways that only a fellow rugby player might notice. He appeared to me, as he stood back from the hug, more reflective and hesitant.

"What time is it?" he asked, looking at his watch, as if to make conversation. "Ah, eleven forty-five," he continued, without waiting for an answer. "Listen, Billy. Why don't *you let me buy you lunch? Let's walk down to the Havana. There's something I need to talk to you about."*

I agreed. "I'll have to call my wife first," I said, which I did. I wasn't going to pass on a free lunch with an old scrumbuddy but, even more so, as I said, he had indeed piqued my curiosity. The Havana it was!

2
Bark Lady

The Havana is really yuppified, which offends my memory of myself as a bona fide Commercial Drive hippie, but then I'm now a yuppie myself, aren't I? – anybody who calls his office a "boutique" has no defence – and, sitting down at a table, I felt right at home.

The thing about the Havana menu is that some of the items read as long as an encyclopedia. Take the Third Beach Bowl: spinach, quinoa, cucumber mint purée, chickpeas, roasted cauliflower, compressed cucumber, avocado, radish, gem tomatoes, candied sunflower seeds, green goddess dressing.

"Green goddess dressing," for God's sake, I mean, for Goddess's sake! And if you don't like it, you can have "mojo

dressing." Mojo dressing? Gag me with a spoon. But I ordered the Third Beach Bowl anyway.

Jack, while muttering about tacos and enchiladas, chose the Little Havana Lunch Bowl and added Spanish chorizo. For a guy named Lewicki – Italiano? Polski? no idea – he sure knew how to eat Latin.

He took an extraordinary amount of time making up his mind about what to choose, and I knew it had nothing to do with the food.

He finally opened his mouth.

"Billy," he said, "It was great luck bumping into you. I have to talk to someone about this, but I don't want to be laughed at or shouted down. I need someone who can listen and will believe me, or at least consider believing me, and I can't think of anyone better than you… and that's a compliment."

He looked right at me, challenging me.

"I'm flattered," I responded, "but naivety isn't my thing. I'm trained to be skeptical."

"But what's he talking about," I wondered. "Was he going to tell me he's undergoing a sex change?"

"I don't want naivety," he said, "quite the opposite."

Looking back at him, all I could do was nod, and with that single nod of mine, as if I were a conductor raising his baton to prepare the first violinist for the opening of a symphony, he began.

I was doing some hiking and wild camping around Pemberton, in the Cayoosh Range to be exact. Heavy duty stuff. I was carrying about 55 pounds. A bit of the way up,

I spotted a crevice I had never noticed before. It seemed just about big enough for a man to squeeze through. Well, you know me, never one to resist a wilderness temptation, so I took off my pack and edged my way in.

It was a tight fit, but I was able to move forward sideways. There was no way I was going to stop as long as I could proceed. A hiker is no match for the power of a crevice. I inched forward more, and then more. "This is madness," I said to myself, which only drove me to keep going. Then, all of a sudden, I saw a pencil of light, then gradually more light. Amazing! I don't think I've ever been so excited, and given my previous adventures, not to name any particular woman, that's saying a lot. I was going to get all the way through in the middle of a mountain! And that's exactly what happened. I didn't even ask how it was possible. I stepped out into full light.

There, in front of me, was a town, or maybe a city for all I knew. I stumbled into the nearest street, stunned. I had difficulty staying on my legs. There were streetcar tracks on the road. I was completely disoriented, also frightened as hell. Jack Lewicki frightened! Can you imagine? I turned around, and the exit from the crevice had disappeared. I was looking at a cliff. "Oh, no!" I shouted out loud. "Now I'm really screwed!"

I didn't want to sit down because I felt, if I did, I'd never get up again. I tried breathing deeply, expanding my diaphragm, and staggered down the street. There were people, now, all looking at me strangely as they walked by me. "Fuck 'em," I said. The buildings were mostly five or six storeys high, staggered in height and staggered in arrangement off the street. Most of the spaces at ground level had shops in them. A streetcar went by. It could have been Toronto. "Face of the Cliff" the streetcar said. A streetcar named Face of the Cliff!

Then suddenly I felt sick. I had thought again of my backpack, an Arc'teryx, expensive as hell, which I had no way of seeing again. Fortunately, I had my wallet with me, with my credit cards and driver's licence, but try as I might to use that thought to cheer myself up, my nausea persisted. I saw a shop sign. "Not the Face of the Cliff," it said. I took that as a sign beckoning me personally and walked in.

The shop was full of custom clothing made, it appears, out of remnants of every kind of imaginable material. The woman behind the counter was snub-nosed, frizzy-haired and black as coal. She was wearing a cute, short dress, made out of bark cloth.

"You look lost," she said, smiling.

"PTSD," I shot back.

"You must have come in through a fissure" she said.

"I don't do fissures, I do crevices," I retorted stupidly. I wanted to be rude. Rudeness was the only weapon I had for fighting my predicament.

She didn't take offence. She laughed good-naturedly.

"Where am I?" I asked, refocusing.

"You're in Pemberland," she said.

"Pemberland?" I replied angrily. I was almost shouting. "Where's Pemberland? Who the hell has ever heard of Pemberland?"

"Only the 100,000 people who live here," she said.

"One hundred thousand exactly?" I asked, as sarcastically as I could. "You've counted them all?"

"Well, maybe not exactly. You're probably something like number 99,993. Maybe even 994."

"If I'm not number 100,000, you can go fly a kite."

This had no effect on her. Her calmness spoke for itself. "I know why you're being so stupid and ornery, you asshole," it said. "You're in shock."

At that very instant, that very nano-second, I don't know why, maybe it was because of the way she was looking at me with her deep brown, almost black, eyes, I settled down. "My Bark Lady," I thought. I felt, all of a sudden, that somehow I could confide in her. Do you know what I mean? How that happens? It goes to show how much of a shock I had suffered.

"We've never had a number 100,000," she explained, "and probably never will. It's theoretically possible, but since there is no way we're ever going to go over 100,000, number 993 or 994, a few numbers below the limit, seems a good place to stop."

I wasn't even going to try figuring that out. I had run out of steam.

Jack stopped there. He looked at me to see how I was reacting. I returned the look with as blank and innocent an expression as I could. I had promised to listen to him, and a promise is a promise. Besides, I was intrigued.

Our food arrived. We spent the next twenty minutes eating and chatting. I tried talking to him about the

Canucks, to divert him – the Canucks were doing well for a change – but I could see the words were going right by him.

"We'd better order coffee," Jack said. "I've only just begun."

We placed the order.

"What do I do now?" I asked Bark Lady, my willpower up the chimney.

"The first thing you need to do is to get a place to live."

"A hotel?" I asked.

"No. Nobody in Pemberland bothers with a hotel. I mean a place to live."

"So I look up Craigslist?"

"You're in Pemberland now, Jack," she said. How did she know my name? "There are no residential listings for Pemberland on Craigslist. I'll take you to Mr. Dindonkey. He'll look after you."

"Dindonkey?"

"His family name is Dinwoodie, but we call him Dindonkey because… well, hmmm, because he's such a hard worker."

She wasn't telling me the truth. It was plain as day.

"Just give me a minute to turn the door sign over and lock up," she said.

3
Dindonkey, Director of Housing

She escorted me to Dindonkey's office. We hopped on a streetcar that happened to be passing by, although the office, she told me, wasn't that far away. The streetcar was free. Her bark-cloth dress next to me radiated a light cedar fragrance, kinda nice – better than Chanel Number Whatever and a lot cheaper.

Despite the novelty of riding on the streetcar, my mind was pulled back to something she had said in her shop. I needed "a place to live," she had said. A place to live! Did that mean I was going to live here in Pemberland whatever I did, that my life had changed, that someone or something had changed my life for me in a mere few hours? I had the sinking sensation I was being carried downstream in a canoe without a paddle, or without a pole, or without even a pee-vee that I could use to hook onto something.

And it wasn't just my backpack that was left behind. There was my car and my job, everything. People would be asking what had happened to me. How could I just disappear? It was a good thing I wasn't married and had kids. I would be screaming, I imagined. Yet so much had changed already, just like that, I couldn't get a handle on it.

I decided that until I managed a better fix on the situation, I might as well just let myself be swept along by the current after all. What did I have to lose that I hadn't, only that morning, lost already?

"Do you have any tips for me," I asked her when we arrived.

"Try not to ask any questions," she said, with a wide grin on her face.

"Why is that?" I queried, noticing the mischief in her voice.

"You just asked a question," she laughed. "Good luck!"

The office was on the third floor. The door was marked:

LANCELOT DINWOODIE, MOH, SPS, TDB
Director of Housing, City of Pemberland
Asking questions is not recommended.
Please wait for the green light before entering.

Since the square light beside the door was green, I walked in.

Dindonkey did have an equine face. There you go. He was in shirtsleeves, a pin-striped shirt, together with a sleeve garter on each arm to help keep his cuffs clean, looking like one of those railway-station agents I remembered from old photographs. The name Pacific Great Eastern flashed through my mind. Past God's Endurance flashed through my mind. Prince George Eventually passed through my mind. Please Go Easy flashed through my mind. Is that where Dindonkey came from, some long-gone PGE station?

He was sitting at a big oak desk, with nothing on it, however, but a laptop. There wasn't even a phone in sight. The place looked stark. The coldness of it made Dindonkey look important. There was a tower beside the desk, like a desktop-computer tower but larger, with an opening in it. On top of the tower was a printer with a V-shaped out tray.

He gestured to a single chair facing him, and I sat down.

"You must be wondering what a director of housing is doing with a chore like this, and no secretary or receptionist manning the gate. It's because I'm efficient and I don't waste time. I hope you got that. Now, what's your name, please?"

I had indeed wondered exactly that, being sent to the big man himself, the director of housing no less, but I gave him my name anyway, Jack Lewicki.

"Lewicki, Jack. Here you are. Resident 99,991.

"Just 991?" I blurted out, offended.

"Eeeyaah." Well, that's what I thought he said. It sounded like a donkey braying, but he quickly suppressed the sound by slapping himself on the mouth.

"How many bedrooms do you want?" he asked sharply.

"One!" I barked back, trying to imitate his so-called efficiency.

He pressed a couple of keys on his keyboard. The printer whirled and shot a paper plane at me.

"There you go," he said.

I just had time to glance at it and see that it contained words when, pfffft, a set of keys flew out of the tower and landed unerringly in my lap.

"Your time's up," he said. "Two minutes. Goodbye."

I was flabbergasted.

"Wait, wait, what rent do I have to pay? You didn't mention the rent."

"Eeeyaah, eeeyaah," came back at me, but this time unrestrained. I thought I saw his nose quivering.

"And don't I even get to choose the neighbourhood I want?"

"Eeeyaah, eeeyaah," this time with more force.

I somehow realized what was happening. If I asked a question, he would start braying. He was Dindonkey! No wonder Bark Lady advised me not to ask questions. But knowing what I knew now gave me a certain power, some control, the first time since I had exited the goddamn crevice. I couldn't resist.

"If I don't know the rent, how am I going to know if I can afford it?" I asked. How do you know I'll be able to pay it?"

"Eeeyaah, eeeyaah," now reverberated in the office and bounced off the walls, on schedule. "Eeeyaah, eeeyaah," more and more fiercely this time.

"And what I really want to know is what do MOH, SPS, and TDB stand for." I threw this out mercilessly, pressing my advantage.

By this time Dindonkey was off his chair and coming around the desk at me. "Eeeyaah! Eeeyaah!" rode the air. The whole building was shaking. It must have been timber construction and could wobble with the stress. If it had been rebar concrete, Dindonkey would have blown the building down, like a tower going down on 9/11. I amscrayed as fast as I could manage. I could swear, as I ran out, he was on all fours, with his head indignantly bobbing up and down, but maybe that was just my imagination, given everything I had gone through that day and the shock I had undergone.

Outside, in the hall, two people had been waiting. They were crouched down on the floor, pressed up against the wall, with their arms over their heads. I caught a backward glimpse, as I flew out, of the red light beside the door changing to green. Dindonkey wasn't allowing a fit of braying to reduce his efficiency. Amazing! And it was suddenly as quiet, now, as the grave.

I thought of my rugby nickname, Jackass Lewicki, but Dindonkey was a real jackass. I, on the other hand, was bray-free. I only swore and shouted.

Seeing Bark Lady waiting for me across the street, I suddenly felt guilty – well, for at least a few seconds. I shouldn't have gone for the jugular the way I did with that last question. On the other hand, a game is a game. Bark Lady and a small crowd that had gathered around her were all smiling.

"You didn't follow my advice," she said gleefully, "but I knew you wouldn't. You can always tell. When somebody like you shows up in Pemberland, we can hardly wait for the showdown with Dindonkey. It's like watching a fireworks show, but with sound instead of sparkles. Eeeyaah, eeeyaah." Her braying was uncannily on key. "And you're such a Vancouver innocent. You don't know the half about him. C'mon, let me buy you a Pembershake triple-delicious with all the works and get some sugar into your system. You could do with it."

4

Jack Discovers What His Rent Is

With Bark Lady's instructions, I made my way to my new residence without any trouble. The free streetcars helped. Once there, I was able to look more closely at the paper airplane.

The apartment, by the way, was quite comfortable, with some furniture and kitchen things to get me started, including a basic bed and a set of sheets and blankets. There was even some food in the fridge, oranges and yogurt, if you call that food. The kitchen had all the modern appliances. There was also, I found, some spare men's clothing in a dresser drawer. Value Village came to mind. The clothing and the dresser were in a competition for which one looked more used and worn than the other. I was still impressed.

The instructions on the paper airplane were brief and to the point:

1. You are responsible for all utilities.
2. The rent is $600 a month.
3. For method of payment, damage deposit, maintenance, social-club contact, and all such other business and social matters connected to your apartment, see the placard on the inside of the walk-in bedroom closet.
4. The first month's rent will be deferred for six months, helping you to get established.
5. To find a job if you need one, please see the current City of Pemberland General Secretary of Finding a Job, Mary Straightarrow, at whatever location she happens to be using at the moment, or look for a damned job yourself, because Ms. Straightarrow won't care a hoot, and you're free to be as foolish as you want, and if you end up in a dead-end job like property development or car sales, you'll only have yourself to blame, and remember above all that the City of Pemberland and its Director of Housing, the esteemed Lancelot Dinwoodie, accept no responsibility for the job-finding advice given in this notice, so there is no way of your being indemnified in the courts pursuant.

That was all, just the one page. No forms to fill out, at least not yet.

I turned over the page from habit. It had a drawing of a donkey on it with an expression of total disdain. Whoever the artist was, that's not an easy thing to do with a donkey, but they succeeded. One of the legs of the donkey, moreover, was raised, not suggesting it was going to piss on someone from a great height, but rather giving me the finger. Since a donkey doesn't have cloven hooves, that's not an easy thing to do either, but the artist pulled that off as well.

Son-of-a bitch. Dindonkey got the last bray on me. I smiled at the thought. "Good for him," I said out loud. I was almost beginning to think of him with affection.

5

Yogi Rasputnik Goorvonovitch

I didn't get much sleep that night. It wasn't because of the bed. It was my discovery of the rent. How could it possibly be only $600 a month? There must be some trick to it, I thought. Mostly, though, I figured that if I found out how they managed rents that low, it would answer all of my questions about Pemberland. With that alone, I might figure out what the hell it was all about.

So my mind raced all night. I had nightmares of paying rent by oozing blood, the rent steadily going up and my blood gushing out, $1,500 a month, $2,000 a month, $3,000 a month, it wasn't stopping! I woke up in a sweat, realizing that it had been just a dream and I only had to pay $600 a month after all. What a relief, I can tell you.

I cut up an orange and ate some yogurt to fortify myself and headed out to see Bark Lady and get the answers I needed. It was easy to find my way back. I just had to look for the streetcar named Face of the Cliff, and it would take me by her place. I needed a phone, I realized, so the next time I wanted to talk to her, I could just call.

Rather than giving me the answers I wanted, or even trying, Bark Lady sent me to a yogi instead.

"Are you kidding?" I objected. "We don't have yogis in British Columbia."

"We do in Pemberland," she said, "but you can relax. He's a friend of mine. His name is Rasputnik Goorvonovitch."

"Rasputnik *what*? What kind of name is that?"

"Yogis have their own names, like everyone else," she said, amused. "You just have to get used to it."

I arranged to have dinner with her that night, at her expense since I didn't have a job yet, and headed out.

I found Rasputnik What's-His-Name in a studio loft. He was sitting alone in a strange, modernistic rocking chair with his knees bent in front of him on a pad, instead of sitting on a bed of nails. Overhead was a skylight. The radiant light would have made him look angelic, but he was anything but. He was swarthy, with dark, bushy eyebrows to match. His hair was like an erupting volcano, slithering down to just below his shoulders. It reminded me, once as a kid, seeing a picture of Mount Etna in full flow. A beard fell to below his waist. The last touch was a downward sloping handlebar moustache.

He was wearing sweatpants and a sweatshirt, probably Pemberland rip-offs of Lululemon, I thought cynically, not that I would be seen dead myself wearing Lululemon stuff, real *or* fake.

In front of him was a narrow birch table with a cup of tea, and off to the side a samovar. There was a similar table for me, also with a cup of tea, but I was left to stand.

Friend Rasputnik seemed to be in a meditative trance, tilting back and forth on his gimmicky chair like a rabbi rocking back and forth, on his feet, in prayer.

"How am I going to learn anything from this guy?" I asked myself. "If he said anything, I would miss it because I would be watching to see if he would lose his balance and fall on his face instead." Or maybe the idea was to hypnotize me, since I had entered his space, and leave me with more ideas in my head than I had wanted. I dunno. But I can tell you one thing: This guy was creepy. I didn't care if he was a friend of Bark Lady's. Creepy.

The so-called yogi never did lose his balance, although he had me catching my breath once or twice. It was something about the chair. Self-balancing. And as it slowly came to equilibrium, it radiated a sense of eternal peace, which is what equilibrium is, right? It was like watching a plumb line coming to rest.

That was the signal for me to ask my question. I put it to him point blank, trying to get across its cosmic importance.

"Yogi, tell me," I said, "how is it possible that the rent for my spiffy new apartment is only $600 a month?"

"Ah, comrade," he began. "I am the great yogi Rasputnik Goorvonovitch. I first explain, yes? I open soul. Many Kashmir yogis. Many Bhutan yogis. Many, many Nepal yogis. Himachal Pradesh yogis. Uttarakhand yogis. But only one Russki yogi, me, the great Rasputnik Goorvonovitch." He jabbed himself in the chest.

"The spirit of Rasputnik Goorvonovitch go back far, back far, far, far back." He held out his arms. "Ancestors. Holy ground of Rusha. Earth, iron, fire, sledge, steam into the sky. Great, great, great grandpapa, Irish mister, Sean O'Reilly, Celt, brave, strong, come to Rusha to build railroad. Marry Yelizaveta, great, great, great grandmamma, babooshka. Me, Innokenti O'Reilly, change to Rasputnik Goorvonovitch for professional reasons."

He leaned forward in his chair to make the point, which disturbed his equilibrium. I had to wait again. The moment he came to rest, I intervened.

"All very nice," I said, like a good little boy, "but you haven't answered my question about the low apartment rent."

He nodded, and then stared over my shoulder, and then up towards the ceiling.

"I search for vision, *tovarisch*," he said into the ether, meditating or pretending to meditate. Time passed. "Yes, I have vision," he began again. "I now see. Dark vision. Terrible vision. Wait. Wait. A traffic jam, India somewhere. Delhi. Can be Bengaluru. Cars, three, four, five, six, seven, eight, ten wide. Motorcycles, a sea, no spaces, overflow between cars also. Ants. Long distance. Forever distance." He put a hand over his eyes as if physically trying to look. "Traffic jam start in Sodom and go to Gomorrah. No move. Like death. They poison. Each one poison other. Terrible."

I was about to interrupt, to try to force him to get to the point, but before I could say anything, he held his hand up to stop me.

"I open soul to spirit, I let wash over me," he carried on. "Ah, ah," he cried out, "I see but no want to see, must look but no want look, but must, must, my duty, duty of yogi. Town, whole town burning, flames rising, smoke rising, I think can touch," he reached out sideways, "but far away at same time, in Other World, town gone, poof. Like that. Poof!" His hands flew upwards into the air. "And another. I see another. People running, but flames catch. And another. And another. Keep coming. Fire and stone. The spirit punish!"

The Russki was getting on my nerves. The guy was a joke, calling himself a yogi and telling me about fires I already knew about without the benefit of even a big, fat joint to remind me, and avoiding my question. When I tried again to interrupt, however, he stopped me the way he had before.

"I see millions, millions, on hands and knees," he was now raving, "slaves, digging in hard ground with fingers, bleeding and moaning, shrieking to curl blood, cries from their mouths, millions, a plague of cries entering bodies of people, entering minds of people, people in all world, your body, *camarade*," he pointed at me, "your mind, *Kamerad*, cobalt they shriek, lithium they shriek, neodymium they shriek, dysprosium, terbium, praseodymium, tellurium—!"

"Enough!" I shouted, trying to shut him up.

It worked. He did stop talking.

"You're a charlatan," I followed through in disgust, taking advantage of the silence and denouncing him with as much authority as I could.

He thought about it.

"No Charleston," he said, quietly this time, his eyes looking beyond me. "I say one time, only one time, Rasputnik Goorvonovitch no Charleston."

"Not Charleston, *charlatan*," I pressed my point. "You were supposed to explain to me why my rent is so low and you talk to me about traffic jams in India, for God's sake."

He considered this, too.

"I already explain, *camarada*," he said. "I have explain. You must listen to yogi, open soul to yogi, but you, not ready. Do not listen. Yogi has name: 'traffic-jam power.' Look at Toyota..." He pointed and pretended to be looking at a supposed Toyota, in his mind's eye, and I was supposed to find it, too. "...GR Supra, six speed manual, three litres." He raised his eyebrows and paused, as if to ask if I was following, the clever bugger. "Toyota in traffic jam Mumbai," he went on. "Three weeks pass. Six weeks pass. And look now. Rents climb to sky. Hong Kong, San Francisco, Vancouver. Traffic-jam power. But not Pemberland! Pemberland trick traffic-jam power."

And with that, he struck his tea table with the edge of his hand, shattering it into fragments and sending his tea and teacup flying.

I had planned to stomp out but, I confess, he now had me mesmerized.

"You early stage, young *kamrat*" he began again. "But I not abandon. I send you to Minister of Finance. He speak different from yogi. You understand. You find at All-You-Can-Drink Golf Club."

"Sounds like the kind of golf club I should join," I tried joking. "Nine holes or eighteen holes?"

"One hole. All-You-Can-Drink Golf Club is bar."

"All the better," I tried again.

"Juice bar."

I tried like hell to think of a comeback for that one, too, but failed.

The yogi looked up into the skylight.

"Is now eleven o'clock. Minister of Finance at golf club one in afternoon. You blessed by gods. Is right day. Minister answer all questions from people. Also buy drinks for people. 24 Main Street. Rasputnik Goorvonovitch call ahead, let Minister know. All-You-Can-Drink Golf Club, one o'clock, *compagno*. Good fortune."

He pressed his hands together in front of his chest, the prayer gesture from yoga. I didn't think it was a Russki gesture, but it was better than being given the finger.

6
The Minister of Finance

I strolled around town for a couple of hours, always curious to see more of Pemberland and hoping the juice drink the Minister of Finance was going to buy me had enough banana and acai berry in it to pass for lunch.

I had barely made my way into the All-You-Can-Drink Golf Club when he arrived. At least I thought it was him.

"Supply and demand, surplus and deficit, income and expenses," he boomed, chortling, his voice such a deep bass that, for a second, his shape changed into a tuba before resolving back into a man.

"Assets and liabilities!" the bartender shouted back, raising a hand cheerfully in greeting. "How are you doin', Sebastian?"

The Minister of Finance only smiled, but such a broad smile that it embraced the room and couldn't help but lift spirits. Nobody else in the bar took notice of the weird greeting.

He spotted me and walked over beaming.

"Sebastian O'Reilly, Minister of Finance," he boomed, pumping my hand. "You must be Jack Lewicki."

O'Reilly? Where had I heard that name before?

"Cash flow, cash and cash equivalents!" the Minister exclaimed brightly, out of the blue, turning into a tuba and back again as he did so. You might have thought he had just won a lottery.

"So you're new here, Lewicki," he continued. "Well, it's the third Thursday of the month, when I, as Minister of Finance, drop in to the All-You-Can-Drink and buy anyone who shows an interest in the public accounts all they can drink. I can afford it because so few people give a damn." He laughed. "If I ever run into someone who gets as far as the Significant Accounting Policies, I'll die of shock." He laughed again. "Now what can I get you?"

I looked at the menu. The smoothies would be more substantial than the pressed juices, I thought, but there were fifty or so, and most had tempting he-man names, so it was hard to choose, names like Raspberry Renegade, Mango Mauler, Green Gargantuan, and Crocodile Classico. Oh, oh, was I supposed to say he-man *and* she-woman names? Anyway, I opted for the Blueberry Boomerang Bam, because it had bananas, whey protein, and frozen yogurt in it, which sounded nourishing. I had never had a smoothie before in my life.

"Excellent choice," the Minister said. "I'll join you."

He called out to the bartender: "Two Blueberrry Boomerang Bams, accounts payable!"

"Two Blueberry Boomerang Bams, accounts receivable, coming up" the bartender replied.

The Minister led me to a table.

He was dressed in a light beige suit, striped shirt and blue and gold patterned tie, like someone out of GQ. It made him look like an important and serious man, but only sort of. You could also take him for a clown. He was fair-skinned and blond. He seemed to be blushing all the time.

He opened the conversation before I could get a word in.

"Over the last few years, the relationship between non-financial assets and net liabilities has remained stable," he said enthusiastically, the image of a tuba appearing again for a nano-second.

"What the hell is he talking about?" I wondered.

"Contractual obligations that commit the City of Pemberland to make certain expenditures for a time into the future are required to be disclosed," he went on, raising his voice a notch.

I just stared back. How had I got myself trapped at a table with this guy? He was plain crazy. I could see, too, he was already growing impatient. He began squirming in his chair. He was going to say something, but didn't. I noticed he was deep breathing, inhale, exhale, inhale, exhale, trying to get whatever was on his mind under control.

Suddenly he blurted out, right at me, "Y equals F times K and L, where K and L are the factors of production, F is technology, and the output is Y!"

He looked at me with his shoulders forward and his eyes full of expectation. I knew I had to say something, but what? I searched around for a thought that sounded important.

"Concrete is made with sand, cement and navvy jack, in whatever proportion you ask for," I volunteered.

His mouth opened wide in surprise, then closed as his head sagged. His shoulders fell. His face fell. How could what I said cause that kind of reaction?

He eventually pulled himself together.

"You don't understand," he said. "Hell, I might as well tell you. Everyone else knows. My name is Sebastian O'Reilly and I am an addict."

It was the last thing I expected from him, but I still didn't understand.

"If you're an addict, what are you doing in a juice bar?" I asked, making things up on the go. "It's not the usual place for getting hooked."

"Oh, no!" he cried. "I'm not that kind of addict. I'm the Minister of Finance. That's how I became addicted. I'm addicted to words from the public accounts. I keep going back to them, although I know they're nonsense. And the more I resort to them, the deeper into my addiction I dig myself. I just can't help it. It's like stuttering."

I decided that the best strategy was not to respond at all, and he would be forced by the silence to keep on talking.

"After a while, not even the public accounts satisfy my craving," the Minister carried on. "I move onto harder stuff I know will fry my brain cells. I'll try economic equations, but their effect lasts for only a few seconds. Almost as soon as I've said one, it becomes irrelevant. What was that equation I just told you? You see, I've forgotten it already.

"And now I'm a figure of fun. Take Alessandro, the bartender, taking my order and shouting out "accounts receivable," right out of a consolidated statement of assets. They play along. They mean well, but how do you think their feeding my addiction back to me makes me feel?"

He began silently crying. I thought I saw, for a split second, a violin where the Minister had been, with the bow moving across the strings by itself. I thought, in fact, I actually heard it playing, squeaking away at the very high end, eeeeeeeeeee, but I couldn't say for sure. Where had the tuba gone?

"Oh, woe is me, woe is me, my friend," the Minister uttered in fragments between his sobs. "The consolidated financial statements," he implored desperately, "have line item after line item, each of which needs careful attention."

Talk about a look of defeat. I could barely keep my eyes on him, he was so pathetic. At that point, our buddy Alessandro showed up and handed us our smoothies, acting as if everything was perfectly normal.

I guess this Minister of Finance thought I should feel sorry for him, but I'm not that kind of guy. I'm for action. I remembered some of our rugby crew who snorted cocaine, you'll know who I'm referring to, and there was also the blindside flanker who was probably on steroids, I'd bet the house on it, you know who I mean, him, too. No use telling them that if they continued, their balls would fall off or they'd go cross-eyed. I couldn't be bothered anyway. If somebody wants to sniff the stuff and it improves their game, all power to them.

This Minister, though, with his blubbering, I took as a challenge. It brought out the game in me, and I had nothing else planned for the afternoon.

"Can I give you a word of advice?" I asked him.

He nodded. A cello also nodded.

"Don't even try to break the habit by holding back," I told him. "It won't work. What you have to do is get to the bottom of it. What really caused your addiction to begin with? Way down deep?"

Then I had another thought, and threw it out as well.

"You've got to get in touch with your feelings," I said.

Jack Lewicki said that? Where did that come from? Must have been something in the air in the juice bar or maybe some blood thinner in my smoothie. What the hell was I doing giving him advice anyway? I don't know anything more than the next guy about addiction.

The finance minister looked up and wiped his eyes with his serviette, and then his lips.

"I know what lies underneath my addiction," he croaked. "I know all too well. I'm not a dummy."

He looked bleak. He jerked his head back as if he were afraid of me, probably afraid I was going to say, "Yes, you are a dummy." I thought he would give up, but he kept on talking.

"Because you're a friend of my friend Rasputnik, and the friend of my friend is my friend, as they say, I will tell you my story, my friend" he said. "In other places, the Minister of Finance is important, maybe the most important person in the government, more important than a prime minister or president, not to mention a mere mayor. Not in Pemberland, though. In Pemberland, the Minister of Finance hardly counts. Everything important happens without me. Nobody needs me or pays attention to me. I could be invisible.

"I am a nobody!"

He wiped his eyes again. I caught a glimpse of a piccolo.

"Do you know why they call me the Minister of Finance?" he asked.

I shook my head like an obedient dog.

'It's because nobody else on City Council would take the finance job, so they offered me a big title to seduce me, and it worked. I liked the sound of it. Minister of Finance…" He spread out his hands in a flourish. "Yes, let me tell you, my friend, do not trust in titles. Oh, they are empty chalices.

"I must have realized this deep in my unconscious from the beginning, but I didn't pay attention. I found myself citing sections of the public accounts without knowing why, and the more I did, the more I did, if you get my meaning. The road to addiction. My title was so empty that I felt driven to do so. 'Attention, attention must be paid to this man, see the public accounts,' I was crying out, but it didn't work. It only humiliated me. I then tried economics, an equation here and there. They just came out of my mouth. It shows you how desperate I was. But they didn't work, either. Economics might be passed off as important in Ottawa or Timbuctoo, but not in Pemberland. In Pemberland, economics doesn't mean squat, as we politicians might say.

"Doesn't mean squat," he mumbled again, reflecting. He raised his eyebrows, as if he was going to ask me a question. "*Ne vaut pas un clou...*" he said. "Heh, heh, a little French there. I had ambitions. A Minister of Finance sitting around a cabinet table. All gone now, into a black hole. All that is left is this hollow husk, this empty chalice, the empty words, the hopeless addict you see before you. Take the low rents people pay in Pemberland..."

I sat up. Low rents! At last I was going to get an explanation. And he had introduced the subject himself. I leaned forward.

"Did I, the Minister of Finance, have anything to do with it?" he continued. "Oh, no. The rents are low because our population doesn't increase. No more than 100,000 people is the rule, and since we had houses for 100,000 a long time ago, the rents are low. *Ergo, voilà,* and Geronimo or, as my friends in IT at the City would say, it computes. Low rents! And do you know who is responsible for that? Who came up with such a diabolical scheme?"

I shrugged to prompt him.

"A weirdo, Willgraph Reesy, called Sir Willgraph, for short. I call him Willgraph Greasy myself. It's not nice, but that's how I feel. He's not even a City Council member. He doesn't have an official position of any kind. The 'Sir' probably came out of a fortune cookie or from a cents-off coupon. He lives in a shack, surrounded by all his numbers like a hermit, and all he knows is air, fire, and water... and, oh yes, earth and garbage. Air, fire, water, earth, and garbage."

He flicked air, fire, water, earth, and garbage away with a flick of his hand.

"I, the Minister of Finance, meanwhile, was pushed to the sidelines, ignored. And, because of his mumbo jumbo, he's got the whole city convinced. If you say, 'Why don't we add another five thousand people to Pemberland?' – a modest proposal after all, indeed a *diplomatic* proposal worthy of a Minister of Finance, I mean what's five thousand people in a world of five billion, ten billion? – people in this city will look at you as if you had gone absolutely mad.

"Oh, I can't stand it. Last week I stopped my gardener, Alastair, and put the proposition to him. A mere five thousand additional people, I explained. 'Interesting, Sebastian,' he replied, 'thanks for sharing that with me, I'll look into it.'

"'Thanks for sharing that with me!' You know what that means, don't you? It means *va-t'en te faire foutre*, if you'll pardon my French again."

He was now on a roll, the words coming at me thick and fast. I tried to remember the name Willgraph for future reference, but it kept escaping me. A French horn appeared and disappeared, in a flash.

"And this guy Alastair looked into it by going to... by going to Greasy himself, of all people!" He spit into a hand to show his disgust. "I've never personally been to Greasy's, but I have an undercover report from one of my staff members on what happens. Greasy overloads his visitors with facts and figures until their heads swim. He takes his time. He will even allow his visitors to stay overnight if they want. He invites questions. *Invites* them! And he enjoys argument, my spy told me. Don't be taken in, though. This so-called scientific openness is part of Greasy's technique to win visitors over, which he does, the bastard.

"The next time I saw the gardener, he said Pemberland doesn't have the energy and water for another five thousand people, or the gardens for them. 'We're already taking up our share,' he said. 'And we already produce our share of something or other in the air,' he said.

"That's not even a proper argument, so how can you argue against it? Air, fire, water, and earth, for heaven's sake. And garbage, for heaven's sake. Greasy has them wrapped around his little finger.

"And there's something else. Dindonkey is in on this. I bet when he found housing for you, he didn't even ask what neighbourhood you wanted to live in."

"How did you know?" I asked, surprised. Dindonkey's bullying still rankled me.

"Oh, I know, I know. Dindonkey maintains a vacancy rate of 10 per cent and an inventory of houses for sale of 10 per cent. He has them spread around the City. It's now official policy. So clever, it makes me weep."

The tears, and the wiping away of tears, began again. "So, you see, it makes no difference where you're settled first. You can change your neighbourhood any time you want, at the same low rent. Young people do it all the time. They try this neighbourhood, try that one.

"'A change is as good as a rest,' Dindonkey says. 'Variety is the spice of life,' Dindonkey says. He has all these cute little sayings he brings up whenever I try forcing the issue. He's another scoundrel. He and Willgraph are a pair, a Subterrene City, I tell you, my friend, right under our feet."

"A what?"

"A Subterrene City, way down below" he said. "A Deep City. Everybody knows what that is."

He stopped to catch his breath. I could see, by his body language, that letting it all spill out and attacking those two guys, Willgraph and Dindonkey, had made him feel a little bit better, notwithstanding his moaning and groaning.

I thought I might help out.

"If there's all that extra housing, surely you can say you should put people in it. Otherwise it's wasted."

"Alas, my friend, alas and alack in spades, we can't exceed 100,000 people. Air, fire—

"Water, earth, and garbage," I intervened, to show I had been listening.

He looked at me suspiciously.

"The vacancy rate is something that Dindonkey added on later," he said. "Dindonkey's vanity."

I tried something else.

"Why not say the extra housing should be made available to immigrants?" I asked. "You can tug at people's heart strings."

"But we have immigrants, my friend. Whatever population space our birthrate doesn't replenish, we fill with immigrants. Except, that is, for a few local Canadians, mostly oddballs, who somehow, through the machinations of the Subterrene City, sneak in."

He looked at me intently to make sure I realized I might be one of those oddballs. I wasn't alarmed. I've been called worse names.

"Our immigrants have been brainwashed by Willgraph, too," he continued. They like him. They think he's protecting them from what they've escaped. They would riot if we abandoned the 100,000 rule, but there's no chance of that ever happening anyway. And Willgraph, the weirdo, claims he's protecting the whole world, too."

That about exhausted my ideas. I had never thought of any of this stuff. I racked my brains for something new.

"You can always look for allies of your own," I hazarded. "Have you tried the Chamber of Commerce?"

"The Chamber of Horrors?" he literally gasped. "In Pemberland, they're the Chamber of Horrors."

We sat there in silence for a few minutes. My Blueberry Boomerang Bam was long gone.

"Well, anyway," I finally said, "you helped me with your explanation of the rental costs. And thanks for the smoothie."

"Did I really help?" he wanted to know.

"Oh, yes."

He looked me over to catch any sarcasm or joking, but I had meant it. He had explained it for me.

He seemed satisfied.

"In that case, I'll accept your thanks," he said. "You're very welcome."

We stood up. Whether it was my thanks or his assault on his enemies, or just his standing up and stretching his pectorals, I could see his confidence ever so slowly building up again, physically in his suit, like an almost empty tank of helium slowly filling up that last balloon.

He shook my hand vigorously. I was surprised he had retained his strong grip.

"The accumulated surplus represents the sum of the current and prior year's operating results and accumulated changes in other comprehensive income," he pronounced, his deep bass voice having returned and the tuba, suddenly back, fading in and out once more where he stood, shimmering with the sound, his voice coming out of the tuba's bell for that quick second or two.

"If you don't pay the stated amount on the invoice within 21 days, we will charge you interest, and if you still don't pay, your debt will be compounded," I replied, joining in the spirit of things without a clue as to what I was saying.

This, too, seemed to buck him up.

Having brushed down his suit with his hands, he strolled towards the exit ahead of me.

"$G_1 + \dfrac{G_2}{1+r} + \dfrac{G_3}{(1+r)^2} + \ldots = T_1 + \dfrac{T_2}{1+r} + \dfrac{T_3}{(1+r)^2} + \ldots,$" he shouted enthusiastically to Alessandro, the bartender, on the way by.

The tuba had appeared and spoken again.

"$E = mc^2$," Alessandro responded gaily. "See you the next time, Sebastian."

And the Minister of Finance, beaming proudly, his back straight, walked out the door with his heart bursting, having had a good fix in the end.

7

Ready-Mix Straightarrow

The next morning, having fattened myself up the previous evening on Bark Lady's dime, I thought I had better get myself a job. I couldn't live for long at other people's expense.

I checked back to the paper projectile Dindonkey had shot at me, having vaguely remembered it had the necessary reference, and there it was: "the current City of Pemberland General Secretary of Finding a Job, Mary Straightarrow, at whatever location she happens to be using at the moment."

"Whatever location she happens to be using at the moment" struck me as not very helpful, but I'm not one to be easily discouraged, so I headed out for City Hall, which was just down Main Street from the All-You-Can-Drink

Golf Club, to get it done. City Hall, it turned out, had a General-Secretary-of-Finding-a-Job self-serve kiosk. I entered an appointment time an hour and a half hence, and the machine not only confirmed the appointment but also informed me where I could find Ms. Straightarrow, at least until the appointment time expired.

I got there in plenty of time. Unlike Dindonkey, Ms. Straightarrow did have a receptionist. The walls of the anteroom were also plastered with framed certificates, suggesting this was Ms. Straightarrow's main office. More to avoid boredom than anything else, I did a tour.

MASSAFORTE INSTITUTE OF TECHNOLOGY
Xana Straightarrow
PhD Whatmakeshumanstickornot

INSTITUT D'ÉTUDES POLYMATHES
Xanaa Straightarrow
Doctorat Etreounepasêtre

INTERNATIONAL ASSOCIATION
OF OPTIC ANALYSIS
Naxana Straightarrow
Global Gold Lens 2015

UNIVERSITÄT GROßER BERG
Axana Straightarrow
Höchste Diplom Maschinelles Gedankenlesen

Those first four certificates were enough for me. I noticed her first name had been spelled differently on each of them and, to boot, "Mary" was on none of them. I wondered if the certificates might be a send-up – Ms. Straightarrow lifting a finger at professionals and the people who hired them, wherever they were in the world, not to mention snotty human resources officers. Still, there was something intriguing about the certificates, even if I couldn't translate some of the words.

After not too long, the receptionist, a boy wearing a denim shirt, jeans, and steel-toed boots, led me into the inner sanctum of The Straightarrow herself.

I had expected, from the name, an upright, uptight straightarrow, with her hair in an upright, uptight bun, but the woman before me was altogether different. She was hefty and well-built up front, with her hair sticking out in every direction. She wore fine leather up and down. What was most surprising, though, was her armour-plating. She had metal armbands – large cuffs – all the way up both of her arms. She also had a choker around her neck with an Indigenous design on it, of an eagle facing off against a bear, a fierce eagle that wasn't going to let the bear push it around. A hammered-copper cummerbund, with another Indigenous design, this one of a war canoe, was around her waist. A small ring hung from a nostril.

All that was missing was an arrow through her hair or, come to think of it, an arrow through her head.

"I wouldn't want to tangle with her," I thought to myself. Then I thought to myself, "I would want to tangle with her!" And then, "She looks like she might tangle with me, too."

"Mr. Lewicki," she said. "What can I do for you?"

"I'm looking for a job," I said.

"Well, you've come to the right place."

Her voice surprised me. It was gravelly, but uncanny, and not only for a woman. You may not believe me, but when I was driving a concrete truck, I could tell by the noise of the drum what was in it. I could even tell if there was too much water in the mix, or not enough, or too much navvy jack for the particular concrete in the drum, or not enough. And I could tell when the mix was the way it should be for the temperature outside. Strange, eh? Vibrations in the ear, like listening to a tuning fork. Well, Straightarrow's gravel voice made me vibrate the same way because it was perfect, perfect gravel, one in a thousand of gravel voices, one in ten thousand. Ever since then I've called her Ready-Mix.

As I was reflecting on all this, she was looking me over.

"First things first, Mr. Lewicki," she said, with that amazing voice, "don't ever think of tangling with me."

I blushed and mumbled, "Well, um, you got me, but you can't really blame me, can you? But how did you know what I was thinking? Everyone in Pemberland seems to know what I'm thinking."

"Mr. Lewicki, are you aware I have a diploma in Maschinelles Gedankenlesen from the Universität Großer Berg in Germany, a rare and valuable diploma, I might add? I'm only one of five such people in the world. 'Maschinelles Gedankenlesen' means 'mechanical mindreading' in English. It's not that I have a machine implanted in my head. The reference is to part of my frontal cortex which engages via neuron synapses, like a clutch, when stimulated by characters like you, not to mention others that might think of playing fast and loose with me or even question what I'm telling them."

I vaguely remembered something in German in one of those certificates I looked at, not that I believed a word she had said or, for that matter, had a clue about what she had said to begin with.

"I see you don't have a résumé with you," she went on.

I shrugged my shoulders.

"I won't even ask why, in your case," she continued. "You deserve an explanation for this, too. I'm not just your run-of-the mill HR robot that depends on résumés to protect their behind. I prefer, in many cases, including outlier cases like yours, to rely on optic analysis instead, an advanced scientific method. I don't like to boast, but over and above my diploma in Maschinelles Gedankenlesen, I'm the winner of a Global Gold Lens, awarded by the International Association of Optic Analysis. To put it in terms you can understand, I "eyeball" people in such cases, eyeball them scientifically.

"I have, in fact, already completed my optic analysis on you, disciplined as I am in doing my due diligence, so I know as much about you now as I need to, without a résumé."

I didn't believe this either. I was sure she was pulling my leg. If, though, I didn't have to produce a résumé, who was I to complain?

"Now, let's get down to the nitty-gritty," she said. "What kind of a job do you want?"

"I'm a concrete truck driver," I said. "Other than some work when I was still a kid that I won't even mention, it's all I've ever really done."

She looked at me fixedly. "Oh, oh," I thought, "more optic analysis, and I don't even have a lead apron draped over me to protect myself."

"Mr. Lewicki, I'm sorry to say—"

"You can call me Jack."

"Okay. Jack, I'm sorry to say there is no demand at all for concrete truck drivers."

"But how is that possible? There is always a demand for concrete truck drivers. Concrete makes the world go round. I can say that as sure as shooting!"

"Maybe in another world, Jack, but not in Pemberland. You see, we have all the housing we need already, including housing for our immigrants, plus an extra 10 per cent for people who like a change of scene. We also have all the sidewalks we need, and community centres we need, and office space, and swimming pools and skateboard parks that we need, that we'll ever need. There's some redevelopment – even reinforced concrete wears out eventually – but not much. Continuing as a concrete truck driver is hopeless."

She paused there to let it sink in. I was speechless.

"I'm going to suggest something else for you" she started up again when she saw I was able to pay attention.

The way she said that, I braced myself for a knockout blow. She had wound me up like a spring.

"Based on my optic analysis and my considerable experience, I think you would do well in home care."

"Home care?" I shouted, almost flying off my chair and bumping my head on the ceiling. "Looking after old people in their homes? You've got to be kidding!"

"I'm quite serious."

"Even if I were crazy enough to try it, I couldn't afford it. I'm not going to take the pay cut. I would want at least $40 an hour, which is what I was earning in Vancouver."

"Listen to me, you stupid idiot," she riposted, catching me by surprise by her antagonistic tone. "I'm not your HR patsy. I'm Mary Straightarrow and The Straightarrow is a straightshooter, have you got that straight? Concrete truck drivers, Jack, just don't get paid very much here because there's little use for them, whereas home care workers have a strong union and are paid well, at least in Pemberland, which is where you happen to be. I hope I don't have to repeat that. It's bad enough I have to say it once."

Her hardware was flashing as she waved an arm to help make her point. The war canoe around her waist quivered, making it look like the spears the warriors were holding were about to be launched in my direction. The ring in her nose swung menacingly.

"What union?" I shot back angrily. "The Hospital Employees Union?"

"The Operating Engineers, Mr. Lewicki. Yes, as it happens, the Operating Engineers. So many unemployed concrete truck drivers began working in home care and hospital housekeeping, they began talking about going back to their old union, and they carried their fellow workers with them. It was a goddamn good thing for the old union's local. It gave them a new lease on life. Otherwise, they would have vanished off the face of the earth."

I was stunned.

She couldn't help noticing. She broke into a big smile, about as warm a smile as I have ever seen.

"Sometimes I have to beat on a person's head to get the blood flowing through their brain," she said.

"I don't know. I'll have to think about it. Give me a day or so to look around."

"Just so you know, I have about fifteen hundred job vacancies in my database, and not one of them is for a concrete truck driver. Actually, I haven't seen one for a long time."

I threw up my hands in surrender.

"I'll jump ahead on this, Billy, to cover this part of the story while I'm at it. Ready-Mix Straightarrow was right. There was no chance of finding work as a concrete truck driver again, as I discovered. And just to get some income quickly, I signed on as a home-care worker, did the training, and tried my hand. It turned out I was good at it. I enjoyed it, too. People liked me. Something about Jackass Lewicki appealed to them. Then I decided to become a nurse. I've done two of four years now. Jack Lewicki RN. It's almost embarrassing just to think about it."

8
Bark Lady Gives Jack a Voice Lesson

As the months flew by, I began to see more of Bark Lady, the first person in Pemberland I had talked to.

Somewhere along the way, we got onto the subject of Dindonkey.

"Just so you know," she said, smiling at the thought of getting a reaction, "I'm a good friend of Din's."

"Don't tell me," I replied. I noticed she had called him Din rather than Dinwoodie or Dindonkey, so they really might be good friends.

She laughed at my grimace.

"You need to understand where Din is coming from," she said. "He's the one who deals with newcomers first, giving them a place to live, newcomers just like you, and if they're from the Other World, they're obsessed with how much their rent might be. It's all they talk about. But it's irrelevant in Pemberland, where rent hardly matters. Din, at first, when he became director of housing and was new on the job, tried explaining it to them, but their minds were so programmed, they couldn't absorb what he was telling them. They would insist it couldn't be done. They'd mention all kinds of silly reasons why, stuff from their brainwashing. It would drive him up the wall.

"Follow me so far?"

"I think so," I said hesitantly. I thought of the housing crisis I left in Vancouver and the explanations we were given for it, that we just needed to build more housing, and how rents kept going up regardless. It occurred to me I myself had been brainwashed. That was why I had been obsessed about finding out why my rent in Pemberland was so low, and why I had gone to Yogi Rasputnik for an answer, and why I had met with the Minister of Finance to finally get the answer when the yogi's blathering just confused me.

Bark Lady had described me – described who I was – down to a T.

"So Din, to save his sanity, worked out this strategy of his. He decided he would give each person two minutes to deal with their housing, not a second more. That was all it was worth. And no questions asked.

"It took a while. The first time he tried it, he used up eight minutes, not bad, something to work with, but far from his target. A lesser man would have been defeated. Din, though, has many talents. Among other skills, he's a techie in disguise. You'll remember the paper-airplane ejector? He built that himself, based on the design of the catapult on aircraft carriers. For the key-thrower contraption, he used an older catapult design, the Roman one used in Mesopotamia in ancient times.

"Through much trial and error, rewriting his ejector software and reformatting the entire inventory database, he got it down to two minutes."

She paused for a few seconds so I could take that in.

"There was, though, still that other problem," she continued, "the questions people kept asking him. He put a notice on the door, saying questions weren't recommended, but that didn't work at all."

"Yes, I remember seeing it." I smacked myself on the forehead. "Oh yeah, you told me, too, don't ask any questions."

"And what did you do, you dodo? You couldn't keep it in." She laughed. "You asked questions which, of course, I knew you would."

She kissed me on the cheek just to make me feel better.

"There was no way, though, once he established his two-minute system, Din was going to waste time and energy answering silly questions. He had suffered enough. He wanted to throw back the stupid questions in people's faces, so he came up with this other tactic. He would bray at them. And the more questions they asked, the louder he would bray. And he had another feeling about it, too, he told me. His two-minute system, on which he had worked so hard – and there is nothing like it anywhere else in the world – was his baby, and if newcomers to Pemberland didn't show his baby respect, they were in for it."

"Okay," I nodded. "I get it, and I guess I haven't done him justice. But that time with me he wasn't just braying. He went berserk. He was a wild man, so goddamn wild he seemed to me to have actually turned into a donkey."

"I know, I know. Yes, I know. Let me try to explain what happens to him, what I think happens, when he goes completely over the edge. I love him, well, love him the way one loves good people. And because I love him, I once brought that very matter up with him, face to face.

"'Don't think I don't know how crazy I get,' he told me. 'It doesn't, in the end, have to do with the people before me and their stupid questions. I keep thinking, instead, of how screwball the powers-that-be in the Other World are, how phoney they are, and worst of all, how they get away with it, ignoring the one thing that could make a difference, keeping their population numbers down. I'm really braying against them, and they're so insufferable, I figure the only thing I can do is to let it all hang out.'

"'Why bother though, Din?' I pursued him. 'Why not just forget about it? It's not our problem.'

"'I'm not so sure,' he said quietly. 'Do you know those famous lines of old English poetry, "No man is an island, entire of itself; every man is a part of the main," or something like that? John Donne was the poet's name.'

"I looked it up and memorized it," she confessed to me brightly, "which is why I can recite it for you now.

"And Din said, 'We're a part of them, too, even if they are in the Other World, and it makes me so sad to see how they're screwing up.'"

Bark Lady and I sat there together in silence for a while, the two of us thinking our separate thoughts.

"Something else good has come of this," she said, breaking the silence. "Braying is now part of stress therapy in Pemberland. You know the idea. When you can't stand something any longer, you go outside and shout as loud as you can until you get the stress out of your system. Well, here, we've added braying to the repertory. Eeeyaah! Eeeyaah!" she illustrated. "Din's braying technique has become fashionable in therapy circles in Pemberland."

She raised her head a notch, all the better to look at me.

"Why don't you try it?" she asked.

"Oh, no, you're not going to deke me into braying like a jackass!" I exclaimed.

'C'mon, Jack, show me what you're made of and, if that doesn't speak to you, just humour me."

She looked at me in a way that only a woman can look at a man. Besides, by this point in our relationship, I was already just putty in her hands and knew I was doomed.

I braced myself in my chair without even bothering to say, "I surrender." I took a few deep breaths.

"Eeeyaah! Eeeyaah!" I hurled into the air.

Bark Lady broke into giggles.

"I'm sorry, Jack, I couldn't help myself." The giggling overcame her again. She finally settled down. "Your eeeyaahs are so anemic. Try again, except this time get some oomph into them. We need more volume. Bring up the air from your diaphragm and project the bray outwards. Pretend that you want to bray the walls down."

"Eeeyhah! Eeeyaah!" I tried again. And once more, gaining in conviction and confidence, "Eeeyhah! Eeeyaah!"

"Better. Much better. You need more nasalization, though, on the second syllable, and you'll have to work on your breathing.

"Eeeyaah!" I gave it another whirl, just one bray, concentrating on my nasalization technique.

She worked on me for a few minutes more. I don't know if you remember, Billy, but I used to sing in the Vancouver Opera chorus when I got a chance so I had experience in following voice instruction. Picking up on Bark Lady's directions was easy.

"Not bad for an amateur," she ended up saying. "Now let's try a duet."

We were off and running, I mean braying. Soon we were doing jazz braying, then something Bark Lady called "baroque braying," a term, she said, she got from the Bray Therapy manual. We brayed and happily brayed, laughing our heads off.

Jack's braying, as he re-enacted the incident, bounced off the walls in the Havana. It was really loud, I mean LOUD! I was totally embarrassed. Sitting at the same table as he was, though, I couldn't very well pretend he wasn't with me. I looked around alarmed, expecting the worst, but all the other customers were pretending they weren't hearing a thing. They were even more embarrassed than I was, or is it that Canadians are so polite, they don't want to make a fuss?

9
Pemberland Annual Bray-Off and Thunder Chorus

One Saturday, sometime afterwards, I was in Bark Lady's shop for close-up. We had vague plans for spending the evening together. After pulling down the blind on the door, she came close and whispered in my ear, "I have a special surprise for you this evening."

I stood back, my blood churning.

"I had been thinking of just such a special surprise for us, too," I said, confessing my own thoughts.

She did a doubletake. Had I jumped to conclusions? My heart sank. I could see her trying to process my comment.

My meaning finally dawned on her, and, glory be, she broke into one of those smiles that lights up the sky.

"That special surprise, too," she said, putting her arm around me. "The surprise I mentioned first is an extra."

It turned out to be a night on the town, the two of us strolling arm-in-arm, like a married couple, to the Pemberland Central Community Centre. Bark Lady was in a bright orange and black wraparound made out of who knows what.

"We're going to a high-society event tonight, Jack, the highlight of Pemberland's social calendar," she informed me on the way. "It's quite exclusive. People give their eye teeth to be on the invitation list. Fortunately, I have influence and was able to sneak you in. I hope you'll be on your best behaviour."

Her eyes were sparkling. I was pretty sure she was pulling my leg.

Arriving at the Centre, we went directly to the room reserved for the occasion. The poster on the easel outside the door announced: Pemberland Annual Bray-Off and Thunder Chorus.

"What are you getting me into?" I gasped *sotto voce* to Bark Lady. "You are positively evil. I should call you the Senegalese Sorceress."

"No, you shouldn't," she joked back. "I've never been even close to Senegal. My parents came here from Alabama. How about Alabama Angel?"

There was already a fair crowd in the quite large room. Dindonkey was there. So was Ready-Mix. Most of the others I didn't know. Dindonkey spotted us right away, or maybe it was just Bark Lady he spotted, but when he came over to us, and after giving Bark Lady a peck on the cheek, he put an arm around my shoulders as if I were an old friend.

"Can I get you a drink, Jack?" he asked. Bark Lady winked at me and was off.

Dindonkey led me to the bowl of Lillooet Lollapalooza Punch and filled two glasses. "I'm sorry I gave you such a hard time when you came to see me," he said.

"Not to worry," I assured him. "Bark Lady has explained it all to me. I do, though, still have a question. What do those letters after your name stand for?"

Dindonkey chuckled.

"MOH stands for Master of Housing, SPS for Superb Public Servant, and TDB for Too Damned Bad. How do you like them? I made them up from scratch, so I'm particularly proud of them. I'd never accept a mere PhD. You have to admit that 'Lancelot Dinwoodie, MOH, SPS, TDB' shows a bit of style."

Not having even a PhD myself, I just laughed with him.

We chatted for a while, after which Bark Lady rejoined us. The gala proper soon got underway. There was an improv satirical sketch mercilessly lampooning Pemberland City Council and anyone else they felt like getting their hooks into. A folk trio gave us a few songs, also with an edge to them. Then the braying competitions began. Dindonkey opened with a ceremonial braying turn. He wasn't eligible for the competitions themselves, since with so much practice, he was deemed to have an unfair advantage.

The Open Category was the most interesting. Ready-Mix, with that unique gravelly timbre of hers, was sensational and won second prize. The copper cummerbund up against her diaphragm didn't hold her back at all.

Anyone in the crowd could nominate additional contestants for the Open Category, over and above those previously registered. Someone shouted "Jack Lewicki." It was, you guessed it, Bark Lady.

"Oh, no," I cried out. "I can't."

This only got the crowd going. By now, they were well-lubricated. A chant went up, "Jack Lewicki! Jack Lewicki!" Soon they were stomping their feet as well. They didn't know me from Adam, but that didn't stop them. Bark Lady was cajoling me, to give me courage.

I had to give in, and the strange thing is, as soon as I did, I felt right about it. There were no butterflies. When I walked up to the raised platform for contestants, I was already envisaging my performance. I looked out at the sea of Pemberlandians and then began. I paid careful attention to my breathing and nasalization, as Bark Lady had taught me, and gave it my best baritone shot. I wound up with the strongest coda I could manage.

I didn't win a prize, but I got a loud round of cheering and applause. It seemed to me they were telling me I was now one of them. Several people patted me on the back.

And something else. Amid the brouhaha, I had this unexpected realization: I was no longer thinking of Vancouver and what I had left behind. I was home in a new world.

After came the finale, the Thunder Chorus, everyone in the packed room, many of us half-lit, braying in unison to rattle the rafters. I thought of all the opera choruses I knew. None of them, including the famous Anvil Chorus with its hammering, was a match for it.

I walked Bark Lady home and we spent the night together as we had planned. The Annual Pemberland Bray-Off – a gala to remember.

10
Letters Shimmering in the Air

My budding friendship with Dindonkey, that followed the Bray-Off, got me thinking. Until Bark Lady had given me the lowdown, I hadn't understood him. I didn't see behind the façade to the wisdom that underlay his peculiar two-minutes-and-your-time-is-up housing system. It occurred to me that I had given old Yogi Rasputnik short shrift as well, back then. There might be more to him than I imagined, and if so, I should get to know him better, too. I might even learn something new. Besides, he was entertaining. And there was one question in particular I thought he would be able to help me with.

So, after mulling it over and procrastinating, I decided to call on him again.

When I arrived, he was in his ergonomic kneeling chair like the last time. The birch tea table with the cup of tea on it was also there –a new table and new cup and saucer to replace the ones he had destroyed the last time. The samovar was there, too. I imagined he hadn't moved since our original encounter – that he had survived all this time by not moving, which would burn up energy, that he kept himself alive with his spiritual reflections, as Russki and absurd as they might be. The routine chores, like replacing the tea table, would have been looked after by a servant, perhaps a devout follower.

He pretended not to see me, looking up into the ceiling of his loft, but it was just part of his act because he addressed me by name at the same time.

"Welcome again to my humble shelter, Jack *Tongzhi*," he said to the heavens, in his best yogi fashion.

I bowed in acknowledgement. I felt silly as hell doing it, but something forced me into it nevertheless. I had just stepped in, and his aura was already getting to me.

"If you don't mind my asking, what does 'Jack *Tongzhi*' mean?" I queried.

"'*Tongzhi*' means 'comrade' in Chinese. You remember last time, you are comrade, also *tovarisch, camarade, Genosse, camarada, compagno*. All mean comrade in different language. Rasputnik Goorvonovitch greet refugees to Pemberland from all countries, practice as many languages as able, to embrace refugee searching comfort here, to show friendship. You here today, I practice on you also, *rafiq*."

I remembered none of this from the last time.

"So you speak at least one word to them in their language, to help them feel at home?" I asked.

"Yes, *malgury*. You hit nail on head. But 'comrade' only first word. Next word is 'citizen,' bigger than 'comrade,' needs many words in dictionary to explain." He stretched his arms wide as he said this, to help show how big the word "citizen" was.

"Is higher level of consciousness," he continued. "Not mean 'You come here, you feel at home,' so simple.' Mean 'You come here, part of Pemberland, not play here today and forget tomorrow.' Different matter than key to door."

He focused on me now.

"No move, *dōshi*!" he instructed. "Let me look. If I have steady gaze, I see into Mister Jack's consciousness. You work hard to open soul to Yogi Rasputnik, so you help."

I just stood there, saying without words, "Here I am." What else was I supposed to do?

After a while, he raised a hand.

"Yes, I can call you now citizen. Citizen Jack Lewicki."

I was moved by this declaration. I didn't for a moment believe he could see into my consciousness, and who was he to give me citizenship anyway, but I recognized he had his own way of doing things, and that was good enough.

I let his words sit for a while and then got to the point of my visit.

"Yogi," I said, "I met with your friend, the Minister of Finance, as you advised, and he did explain to me why my rent is so low. I also know, now, that everyone in Pemberland can afford good housing without any difficulty. This only leads to another question. Pemberland does a lot of things for everybody together, but those things cost money. We even have free streetcars. I never would have imagined it possible until I arrived here. And I've been a home care worker. Home-care workers cost tax money. Yet home care here is far more generous than in the Other World. Everyone has a doctor, too. And hospital beds are always available.

"Yogi, tell me, how can this go on? How can we afford the taxes to pay for it? And another thing: I haven't heard any complaints about all the taxes we pay. Nobody says our taxes should be reduced. This is even more of a mystery."

I could see the yogi struggling with this, probably, I thought, struggling with how to explain a mystery that was inexplicable. He didn't stay silent for long, though.

"I lead you on journey," he said.

I nodded, just the once, to keep him moving.

"I call on powerful spirit, imagination, great power. You join me, show me power."

I nodded again.

"We are on path through forest. Much growth. What you see?"

"I see, um, moss beside path," I responded, thinking fast. "Dried out blackberry stalks. Salal bushes."

"What else?"

"A fern, and there's another one, a giant fern, as big as a box tree," I improvised.

"Now are hemlocks."

"One is a Douglas fir, not a hemlock," I countered.

The damned yogi had got me in full competitive mode and my blood was up. I could have been on the rugby pitch.

"Ah, a Douglas tree? Yes, I see difference now. Tree over there, so high. Some cedars. Which higher, Douglas or cedars? Path runs into big rock. We go around rock."

"Other big rocks, down into a glade."

"Water running. Do you hear water? A little more far. Now look! Look up! A waterfall."

"Quite spectacular!" I exclaimed, although it was actually a modest waterfall. I was challenging him to contradict me now. "A sheet of green water crashing down into a pool below us, with wild orchids on its edge and, wait, I don't believe it, it can't be, a palm tree!"

Yogi Rasputnik didn't rebut my description of the waterfall and its surroundings, or I might have strangled him with a piece of the tropical vine I would have added to the scene for the purpose. He just sat there instead, rocking slightly in his kneeling chair.

I decided to call him to task.

"What does all that have to do with our ability to afford free streetcars?" I asked.

"Nothing," he said, "but isn't waterfall beautiful?"

I understood. I was learning to think a little bit like him. I still, though, wasn't going to let him off the hook.

'That only means you still have to answer my question," I confronted him.

He slowly nodded acknowledgement.

"Before I answer, you must first prepare, must first visit wise colleague Sir Willgraph Reesy, get instruction."

Where did I hear that name before? Then I remembered. The Minister of Finance had mentioned him when I met him, and hadn't hidden his disgust. "Willgraph Greasy," he had called him. According to Yogi Rasputnik, on the other hand, Greasy, I mean Reesy, was a "wise colleague."

"That doesn't cut it," I persisted stubbornly. "I'll make a deal with you. If you tell me how we in Pemberland can afford such good public services *and* free streetcars, and not complain about the cost, I'll visit Sir Reesy the next available weekend I have."

To his credit, the yogi considered this, too.

"So you want to know code for measuring rich prosperity?" he mused.

I threw up a hand to show that was exactly what I wanted to know and he should get on with it.

He took a little bell out of his sweatpants pocket and rang it. A servant arrived promptly from out of the back with a director's chair. He was dressed as a butler, but was wearing sneakers. Except for the sneakers, he was about as different from his master as one could imagine. He unfolded the chair for me and, taking the hint, I sat down. The butler skedaddled.

"You, *Citoyen* Jack, and because you citizen, I make exception for you," the yogi began. "We meditate to find answer. I bring chair to save you sitting on crossed legs. I need *Ciudadano* to be comfortable, loose, how you put it. Now, how we go. We no chant Om. Om sacred. Helps mind and body energize, but not good for question. We chant, instead, Mah-nee. Also people worship and also energize. Must chant slow to create vibrations, slow-slow, chant like ghosts, we chant, become ghosts. I am giving you heads-up as English say, now Russki say, too. Mah-nee…"

And before I know it, the two of us were chanting Mah-nee, really wailing Mah-nee, ever so slowly, stretching it out, wailing like ghosts in some terrible horror movie, *A Nightmare on Main Street*, Maaaaaaaaaaaahhhhhhhhneeeeeeeeeeeeeeeeee. Maaaaaaaaahhhhhhhneeeeeeeeeeeeeeeee. Soon I forgot the body I was in. I felt the room growing dark, slowly, too, so slowly I didn't at first notice it was happening.

Maaaaaaaaaaahhhhhhhhneeeeeeeeeeeeeeeeee.

I don't know how long we chanted because the chant was hypnotic and I lost sense of time. It might have been twenty minutes or might have been a couple of hours. At some point, vibrations of light became visible behind the yogi. And then the glimmering of light began turning into shapes which, slowly, slowly, revealed themselves as letters, unreadable, and then barely readable, Maaaaaaaaaahhhhhhhhneeeeeeeeeeeeeeeee, and then clearly readable.

GDPPCAPPP

I stopped chanting, mesmerized by the apparition, the letters shimmering in the air, not altogether steady. I noticed the yogi had stopped chanting, too. How had we done it, or to be accurate, how had Yogi Rasputnik done it? He had no laptop or keyboard of any kind, nor any projector – no device of any kind, except his little bell – and there was no backdrop, either, for the letters to sit on. Nor could the butler with sneakers have done it. There was no light coming from the back.

"Those are only letters, just gobbledygook," I cried out when I came to my senses. "That's no answer to my question. What do the letters mean?"

"I, yogi, am forbidden to tell. You must go on second journey, journey of life in Pemberland, and discover without yogi. Citizen Jack discover. Otherwise, you just know meaning but not seize it!" With those last words, he raised an arm and clamped his fist to show what he meant by seizing the meaning. "You remember letters and discover. I say no more. I glue lips."

That only raised the question of how I was going to remember the letters. I began repeating them out loud, only to realize I would probably do better if I sang them, which is what I did, singing them over and over again, singing like Pagliacci, the clown in the opera.

And, to demonstrate, he began singing the letters for me in the Havana, rugby-player baritone, which meant kind of shouting. He was bellowing. I was alarmed. He seemed to have gone completely crazy, unaware of the circumstances. This time, however, everybody in the restaurant was openly listening, rather than politely pretending they hadn't noticed. This included the servers, who held themselves back. Finally, Jack, noticing everyone staring at him, stopped, upon which, much to my astonishment, he was given a boisterous round of applause. "Bravo, maestro!" one of the servers shouted, not so much for the singing, I thought, but because of Jack's bravado in performing spontaneously in a restaurant.

And so I sang, and kept on singing, exiting Yogi Rasputnik's loft, out into the daylight and all the way home, until I got there and could write the letters down.

11
Sir Willgraph Reesy

With contact information from Bark Lady, who seemed to know everyone in Pemberland, I made an appointment with Sir Willgraph Reesy for the following weekend, and duly showed up at his place that Saturday morning. Even without my deal with Yogi Rasputnik, I would have eventually gone to see Reesy. It seemed he was the key figure for the 100,000 population limit, or that's what I vaguely gathered from the Minister of Finance and his denouncing of Reesy. Like everything else in life that exercises me, I would want to find out for myself what this character was up to.

The supposed "shack" that Sir Reesy lived in was much larger than I expected. I'd call it a small hangar, large enough for work that needed more space than an office or a basement.

Whether Sir Reesy himself was a weirdo or not, as the Minister of Finance had insisted, his workshop was certainly weird. There were painted lines and bars everywhere – on the walls, the ceiling, the floor, looking like one big modernistic painting in total disorder. "Total chaos," I thought. I was so struck by it, I stood transfixed until Sir Reesy himself approached me.

On the surface, he looked like the proverbial absent-minded professor, his hair mussed, his sweater coming out at the elbows, his eyes bright and open. I noticed, however, peeking out from under a cuff of his shirt, the trace of a tattoo, which caught my interest.

"Mr. Lewicki," he said, shaking my hand. "It's a pleasure to meet you. You can call me Willgraph."

"And I'm Jack," I said.

I stood there, still looking around.

"So, what's this all about?" I asked, sweeping my hand across all the lines and bars. "It looks like a madhouse."

"They're all graphs," he said, smiling with pleasure. "I call this place The Graph Factory. And it is a madhouse, you're right about that, or rather, it's the precise representation of a madhouse. If you would like to sit down, I can tell you all about it. I have some coffee on. Would you like a cup?"

We sat down on a couple of easy chairs in the middle of the hangar, with lines that had come down off the wall and were running on the floor under the two chairs. There was a platter of Arrowroot biscuits on the coffee table between us. I hadn't seen those since I was a kid. The sight of them triggered an instant pang for a chocolate torte with double whipped cream on the side, that I obviously couldn't ask for and, I was quite sure, wouldn't be available even if I did.

"It's a long story," Willgraph began. "My father was a mathematician, a professor of math, a full professor, at the University of Toronto, no less. Somewhere along the line, he began fretting about where the world was going, but like most people working with figures and equations – mathematicians, engineers, and the like – he couldn't get his thoughts together, much less articulate them for other people. If you've been to university, you'll know what I mean – engineering students, math students, the chemistry majors, awkward and clueless when it comes to worldly matters and the meaning of life, whereas the arts students are not only comfortable with such subjects, they figure they know it all even before they graduate.

"And there was my father, the math professor, grappling with his feelings and concerns. The one thing he struck upon that might get them across but still have the purity of mathematics was graphs. I was just coming into the world at that time, so he, with my mother's approval, named me Willgraph."

"Yeah," I interrupted, "parents sometimes go for strange names, never thinking what it might mean for the kid growing up."

"Oh, I didn't mind. 'Willgraph,' for me was a perfectly normal name, and my schoolmates never had any trouble with it, either. Willgraph was just me. And my father was prescient," he laughed. "Just look around you."

Out of habit and to occupy my hands, I had picked up a few of the Arrowroots, but having eaten them, I felt a bit queasy. I sensed a bit of a headache coming on.

"So, explain some of these to me," I said, trying to get my mind off my queasiness.

"Well, let's start with the basic ones," Willgraph started out, getting up and walking over to a whole series of bar graphs on one of the walls. These show the population each country can manage and still be sustainable. Clean air to breathe comes into it. And then fire, how much you can burn without exceeding your quota of CO_2 emissions. Then water. Somewhere I've got California here."

He looked around in the maze of bar and line graphs.

"It's somewhere here. They're running out of water. Well, I can find it later if you're particularly interested."

"Air, fire, water, earth and garbage," I said, remembering the litany about Greasy, aka Sir Reesy, aka Willgraph, that the Minister of Finance had repeated with such disgust.

Willgraph's eye's opened wide in astonishment.

"How did you know? That's good. You should have been a student of mine. Yes, the natural fertility of farmland and forest, and getting rid of all the waste, too, a real problem, because if you try burning waste, you use up your sustainable allowance of fire, that is, CO_2.

"Now, here we come to my masterstroke, a true stroke of genius, if you don't mind my boasting. I call it the Willgraphian Extension, copyright registered, not that I mind other people using the expression. I just don't want them abusing it, and with copyright I can control the use. Do you know those paintings by Salvador Dali with melting watches folding over the ends of tables?" he carried on, changing the subject without a break. "I said to myself, 'Why can't the bars and lines of graphs fold as well?' Dali, of course, if you know the name, was a surrealist. Surrealism – a super reality, a surreality. That suited my purpose, too, because where the earth is going today is altogether surreal. I'm an ecological footprint analyst. Have I mentioned that?

"Anyway, here is the Willgraphian Extension at work. A bar representing population climbs up the wall. The ceiling is as far as it can go within the bounds of sustainability. After that, it folds onto the ceiling just like one of Dali's watches folding over tables and tree branches, and if it keeps going to the opposite wall, it folds down that wall in turn, and then onto the floor and back up the first wall, if it gets that far.

"Now this one" – somehow a pointer had ended up in his hand – "is the global population. The top of the wall, for this bar, is two billion people max."

I followed the bar. It folded onto the ceiling, then down the next wall, then onto and across the floor, and then back up the first wall again, just as Willgraph had explained. And there were umpteen such bar graphs to follow, most of them folding onto the ceiling and some, like the global population, continuing on.

Looking at the bars, I had the uncanny feeling that they were moving. I blinked and then closed and opened my eyes to stop it, but that didn't help. Things that move while you're trying to watch them are bad enough, but when they move only slightly, so slightly you can't even really see it, but you're seeing it nevertheless, is much worse. My nausea was rising. The place was giving me the creeps.

"Now this red line here," he pointed it out, "is the same idea but in a line graph rather than a bar graph, and it reads horizontally as well as vertically, because it shows the change over time. It starts here on the left in 10,000 BCE and then continues through time. You'll see it rising sharply after 1800, with the industrial revolution underway, and then, in the 1900s and later, it just goes berserk."

I carefully tried following the line, which was harder than following a bar. It was flat for the longest time and then went up at a gentle and then increasingly steeper angle until, at some point, it was going almost straight up, onto the ceiling and all over the damn place. And there were lines after lines doing the same thing, in a sickening tangle.

"Did you put poison in the Arrowroots?" I asked Willgraph out of the blue. "I'm not feeling well."

"The Arrowroots? No, it won't be the Arrowroots that are causing you trouble. I munch on them myself."

"Well, then, are the bars and lines moving, playing with my vision? Is that what is doing it?"

He raised his eyebrows, pleased with my question.

"I'm surprised you noticed it. Good, really good. I owe you an explanation."

His voice had softened. He sat down and put his pointer aside.

"Yes, the lines are moving, because the relentless rise in population keeps moving and the level of CO_2 in the air keeps moving. I needed my graphs to capture that movement in real time if they could. A couple of guys at Pemberland City University did it for me, real geniuses, far brighter than I am. I'd explain it to you if I was able, but I'm not. Graphs in real time! They're amazing. We call their action on observers the Willgraphian Kinesis Effect.

"The Willgraphian Extensions and the Willgraphian Kinesis Effect work together, but that's not what's making you sick, either. They're just the messengers. What's making you sick is what they represent. You're not the first to react that way. Look around you."

I dutifully looked around me.

"Do you see those pails in the corners?" Willgraph continued. "They're for upchucking. At first, I felt guilty, making my visitors sick – who would want to do that? – but there was nothing I could do about it. Then, as time elapsed, I realized I really was guilty. I wanted my visitors to get sick. Unless they were as sick as dogs, they wouldn't realize, in their very insides, what a fiendish nightmare all this represents. On paper, in my academic articles, my graphs told the story, but they didn't have the necessary punch, no matter how much I discussed them. The Willgraphian Extensions and the Willgraphian Kinesis Effect do. In my subconscious, that was probably what I was aiming for all along when I originally created The Graph Factory.

"So there you have it. I wanted you to get sick and I'm glad you did. I'm glad you did, because you'll be healthier afterwards."

He said this quietly and matter-of-factly, and with a face so sad I thought it was going to melt like one of Salvador Dali's watches.

"I can offer you some hope, though," he said. "Do you see those two bars in the corner over there?"

He pointed them out.

"The first one goes all the way up the wall to the ceiling, but doesn't quite touch it. That's Pemberland, real-time Pemberland, I remind you.

"The other, which also doesn't touch the ceiling, is Tikopia, one of the Solomon Islands in the Pacific. For over two thousand years, its residents have kept their population stable, for most of that time without the pill or any other such modern device, because they knew their island could accommodate only so many people if they were to survive."

This didn't calm me down. My head was swimming and aching, not to mention my stomach. It was all I could do to try to take in what he was saying. And then, sniffing, I noticed something else.

"I smell smoke!" I cried out. "That's what's making me sick!" I looked around desperately, to see where the smoke was coming from.

"That's only the CO_2 line graph, up there, smouldering. It's already hit the ceiling and is beginning to crawl across it." And sure enough, as he pointed it out, there it was. "The longer it gets, the hotter it gets, and because of the built-in Wellgraphian Kinesis, the whole line gets hot."

"What if it gets so hot that it ignites the ceiling and, I guess, the wall, too?" I asked.

"Well, then, The Graph Factory will burn down – right? – and I'll burn to a crisp with it. I've asked my scientific friends at PCU, the university, to program the line so that I can't artificially alter it."

If a mournful face could look even sadder, his face managed to do it.

"You're still hiding something from me," I said. A wayward thought had entered my head, despite all the upset I was going through.

"What's that?" Willgraph sat up.

"Your tattoo. Let's see your tattoo."

This caught him unawares. I knew tattoos were a personal thing, and how rude and offensive I was in challenging him to show me, but I was in turmoil and I couldn't help myself.

"Are you sure you want to see them?"

I sensed he was warning me I might regret it and he didn't want to take the blame for it.

I nodded.

"Nobody else has ever asked me about them," he said, "but I believe in openness, and I guess there is always the first time."

He took off his sweater, slowly and with care. Then he unbuttoned his shirt cuffs and the front of his shirt, also slowly. Then, with a flourish, he tore the shirt off.

His whole body was covered with bar graphs and line graphs in miniature. It was more than a jungle, it was a bloody morass. In many places, the bars and lines were so dense or the intersections so many, the effect, without a magnifying glass to separate the parts, was blackness. I was stupefied. I couldn't take my eyes away from it. Some of the bars and lines went down into his pants. Where did they begin or where did they end, down there? Then something caught my attention, or did it? I thought I noticed movement, ever so slightly, not really perceptible, turning the morass into a quivering mass, like a bowl of jelly, but then not, because my stare couldn't fix it, and the more I tried to catch the movement in my mind's eye, the more I lost it, so I couldn't be sure it was happening at all.

My stomach now was heaving.

How can tattoos be programmed with Willgraphian Kinesis?

I ran out of The Graph Factory as fast as I could, just making it to the sidewalk before puking my guts out.

12
Jack Gains Perspective

Instead of taking the streetcar back home, stinking with the traces of vomit as I was, I wandered through town until I came across a small park with a water fountain, never so welcome, and a bench I could sit on.

I tried sorting out my feelings.

Right off the top, I was never so glad to be living in Pemberland with its limit on population. That ceiling would be broken over my dead body. The Willgraphian Extensions got to me, alright. I understood now how Pemberland's limit had held and why the Minister of Finance blamed Sir Willgraph for it. You couldn't visit The Graph Factory without being convinced that Pemberland was on the right track, convinced right down to your short hairs.

The Chamber of Horrors wasn't the local Chamber of Commerce, as the Minister of Finance had called it. The real Chamber of Horrors was the surrealistic lines and bars crawling along the ceiling and down the opposite wall, and sometimes back across the floor, in The Factory.

But what of Sir Willgraph? It's remarkable how quickly you recover from vomiting. Out in the fresh air, with my stomach settled, I was already thinking he wasn't such a bad guy. Not more than an hour after running madly out of The Factory, I was actually thankful he had made me sick, I mean his bars and lines had made me sick. "That's what it takes," I said to myself, nodding in agreement. And, what the hell, it was a new experience I could trade on for umpteen coffee sessions.

Even in that short interval, I was also able to get his tattooed body in perspective, stunned as I was when I saw it. Willgraph seemed to be a reasonable guy. He talked calmly about facts and answered questions. And he didn't go flashing his tattoos around. What had driven him to get the tattoos, so out of character with the rest of him? I could only speculate.

He is still alive, by the way, and still doing his work. Pemberland is lucky to have him.

13

Ma Shen Li-ping

By the time I moved from full-time home-care work to studying nursing, Bark Lady and I were cohabiting. The change also brought a problem to mind, a problem that kept niggling away at me. Home-care work is mostly with aging people, although it also involves others who can't look after themselves on their own. If I had left the job, wouldn't at least some of the other care workers be doing the same, so where are all the new home-care workers to come from?

Somehow, maybe from my previous life in the Other World, I had it in my mind that with so many people getting old and retiring, because that's what people do – and I, in time, would become an old person, too – there would be a crisis filling all those jobs that required hands on. Artificial intelligence and all those other high-tech gimmicks wouldn't do the trick. I couldn't get this worry out of mind. It was like having a worm in my brain.

I brought it up with Bark Lady.

"You should go see Ma Shen Li-ping. She's not just an old lady who knows about looking after people and being looked after, she's a really old lady and she's seen it all. If anyone can help you, it will be her."

"So she can remove this worm from my brain, you think."

"Oh, no, she'll blast it out," Bark Lady joked. Or was she joking?

No matter. I was wise to her now and looked around for an idea to cover myself.

"Why don't you come with me?" I proposed.

Bark Lady laughed uproariously. She was clearly wise to my being wise to her.

"No, you go yourself, big guy," she said. "You can handle a little old lady. Besides, my ears are already blue."

"That doesn't sound good," I thought. But Bark Lady gave me such a sexy hug and kiss, that I didn't insist. I could live with blue ears, although I wasn't sure about a blasted brain.

Ma Shen Li-ping, it turned out, lived in a vintage town house. I rang the bell, and after I introduced myself as Bark Lady's partner, with greetings from her, she let me in. Inside, her place was open plan, in effect one big kitchen.

Ma Shen was tiny, short of five feet. She was as old as the hills. I estimated, based on my home-care knowledge of the elderly, she was pushing 100. Her skin was taut over her cheekbones, almost translucent, and there were liver spots on her arms. She looked so fragile, I was afraid that if I sneezed, I would blow her over.

While I was sizing her up, I had the feeling she was doing the same with me, wickedly measuring me for some devious scheme of hers, that having gone through her door, I was a fly in her web.

"Sit your ass down there, young sprout," she said, grinning with anticipation, "and tell me how I can help."

I explained the question troubling me, basically how were we going to find the people to look after those who needed help or care when the people working on such jobs now were eventually going to retire.

"Stupid fucking question," she said. "Well, you motherfucker, if I'm going to help you, you're going to help me."

I learned later that "motherfucker" was one of her favourite opening gambits.

She opened her mammoth fridge and began taking out bags of vegetables, which she put on a long butcher-block table behind her. Other packages joined them, and other bags from a couple of cupboards.

The first item to be spread out on the table was potatoes and, after them, carrots.

"Your first job, dorkface, is to peel these things," she instructed me gleefully, enjoying herself and handing me a potato peeler.

"Excuse me, I don't want to be rude," I said, thinking she probably had dementia and a complete loss of short-term memory, "but how does that help answer my question?"

"Just shut your lip, scumbag, and do what you're told," she replied good-naturedly.

So there I was, kitchen slave labour peeling potatoes, or trying to. She was merciless, a sadist, getting after me for going too slow and calling me names to speed up production. She could have had a whip.

"Do it this way, you snot-nosed stumblebum," she tossed off, feigning innocence. Damned if she didn't peel a potato in a quarter of the time it was taking me, despite her arthritic fingers.

Well, to make a long story short, the two of us worked away, snicker-snack, peeling, washing, slicing, chopping, cubing, shelling, adding to the existing pile onions, celery, green pepper, mushrooms, peas, and God knows what else. From a large pot on a stove top, she had also produced stewing beef which, she told me, she had previously seared and then simmered, and then frozen, and now was also ready to go. Her main cooking appliance, though, was a custom-made apparatus only a couple of feet off the floor, with multiple electric heating elements arranged in a circle, like a fire, and upon which sat a large cast-iron stew pot.

"I was chop-sueyed out by the time my old man died," she explained, "and I took a hankering to stews. Something altogether new for my old age, I decided – continental cookery. I set out to create a new Shen Li-ping. Nobody was going to pigeonhole me. Now pay attention, asshole, here we go."

Having turned the elements on, she poured boiling water into the vat and emptied into the water a couple of cans of beef broth and a can of tomato paste. Then she started in on the vegetables.

"Here go the developers," she said, throwing in a few of the potato chunks.

"Those aren't developers," I blurted out, astonished, "they're potatoes!"

"You can call them potatoes, you stupid prick, but I call them developers. No use for them in Pemberland which is already developed. Then there's the developer's lobbyists, PR flacks, and political friends, and all their assistants and secretaries." Another handful of potato chunks flew into the pot. "Architects, engineers, technical designers, and all of their gangs that work on new developments. Next the morons who work for concrete companies including these," she held up the remainder of the potato chunks, "concrete truck drivers."

I watched my old self go into the pot.

"Now what are these?" she asked me, holding out a bowl. I looked in. They were the carrots. I hesitated.

"Don't you have eyes in your head, you nutcase, or are you just plain blind as a bat?" she kept after me. "Can't you see what they are?"

"Carrots," I shouted, flustered by her badgering.

"Totally wrong, you dildo," she chortled. "They're all the other guys who work on new mega-developments – carpenters, plumbers, electricians, iron workers, rod busters, drywallers, painters, cupboard makers, appliance dealers, truckers…" With each one, and her list went on forever and ever, she dramatically, with a great show, dropped in a single diagonal slice of carrot. She needed to ration them to have enough to last until she got to the end of her list.

"Next is this useless lot," she said, sticking them in front of my nose to identify. They were the onions, on a cutting board.

Having been burned twice, I was prepared now. "She's not going to make a fool of me again," I swore under my breath. No way were those onions onions. I stared at them as hard as I could to force them to tell me what they were. They didn't answer, so I had to put my brain to work. All those non-existent developments in Pemberland, and all those non-existent, unnecessary new condos, would have needed non-existent peddlers to flog them, so I went for it.

"Realtors!"

"Wrong again, dummkopf," she crowed. "These are community planners. Don't you recognize them?"

She began sliding the community planners into the pot, chanting with each swipe as she went along:

"Bunch of lackeys,

"Zoning and rezoning,

"Developers blowing,

"Smoke up their asses."

Boy, was she ever crude, and from me that's really saying something. Still, I did recognize them, now, as they fell into the pot, completely unnecessary so-called planners, since Pemberland had a community plan a long time ago, and it only needed the occasional tweaking.

"These are next, airhead."

She put forward the bowl of peas. Maybe because peas are so small, my looking at them didn't give me the necessary inspiration. I was really bamboozled. I decided to give myself a rest.

"I pass on the… on the… ," I said, holding back the word "peas," and trying to recover my wits.

"Fucking spineless coward," Ma dismissed me. "These are immigration lawyers!"

"But Pemberland has at least some immigrants," I protested.

"Almost all of them refugees and we know they're the most important people to accept," she sniffed airily, putting me out no end. "We don't need lawyers for that."

She had absent-mindedly left one pea behind in the bowl, and by this time I was so pissed off by her arrogance, I pounced on her, pointing an accusatory finger at the pea.

"You left one of them out," I sneered. "Didn't you see it?"

"I didn't leave it out. I'm keeping that one. It's the one immigration lawyer we do have."

"That's not the only one you left out," I counterpunched. "There are all those non-profit people that work with immigrants, the ones who help them with housing, for example. But in Pemberland, Dindonkey looks after them in just a few minutes and also sends them to Ready-Mix for a job. And in Pemberland, even refugees with nothing in their pockets when they arrive can afford everything. I know from personal experience!"

From out of nowhere she produced a jar of bay leaves.

"Here they are" she said, holding the jar up to the light. "Non-profits! Just for you, fuckhead sweetheart."

She took a handful out of the jar, leaving the rest, and floated them one by one into the pot, to show how clever she was.

"Now for the richest part of the stew."

She took the pot of stewing beef, already prepared, off the regular stove top, and held it in front of me.

Although I had passed on the immigration lawyers, I thought I was getting closer with each ingredient and might just have a chance this time. I could almost taste it. The *richest part* of the stew? The *richest* part of the stew? "Money," this said to me, which led me to all the loans that financed developers and all the mortgages on floods of condos with hugely inflated prices. I reviewed my reasoning, step by step. It seemed to hold up.

"Bankers."

I put it out there decisively, but evenly and calmly, like an accountant, to protect myself from one of Ma's comebacks in case I was wrong.

"Bingo!" Ma Shen exclaimed, her eyes wide. "The dildo has a brain after all!"

Into the pot went the bankers.

She took as much pleasure from my success as she did from calling me dirty names. I myself was ecstatic, although I did my best to hide it. It was all I could do to stop from putting my arms into the air. The champion!

We went through the other ingredients, I mean the other unnecessary jobs, in the same way – into the pot. "Bankers" was the only one I got right, but I didn't care. All my wrong answers kept Ma delighted. I could have just repeated "realtors" for each of the additional ingredients and automatically got at least a second answer right, but I wasn't going to stoop that low.

With the working table cleaned off, Ma went to what might have originally been a broom closet and took out an oar, with which she proceeded to stir her stew.

This was ridiculous. The stew pot was oversized, but not that oversized. She obviously wanted to make a production out of it.

"I get the idea," I announced as she stirred. "With all those unnecessary jobs thrown into the pot and not using up people, there are lots of people left for all the jobs that actually need to be filled. I see doctors and I see berry pickers. Everyone we could possibly need. Opera singers, too. Rappers. And, hallelujah, home-care workers. I'm wondering, though, what do economists say about it?"

"Economists? Jesus Christ on a bike, I forgot."

She laid down her oar across the pot, went to a cupboard, and pulled out a jar of a cream-coloured powder. "What does this smell like?"

I sniffed.

"Ah, pungent. It's obviously garlic powder."

"You triple ignoramus asshole supreme," Ma shrieked with joy. "It's ground-up economists." And she threw a couple of healthy spoonfuls into the stew.

"Stupid fucking economists, yattering on forever and drawing circles in the sky," Ma carried on, flushed. "Anal retentive, with their fingers up their watchamacallits, without a stupid fucking brain in their heads. Do you know why the lone economist attempted suicide?"

I had no idea, or as Ma would have put it, no fucking idea.

"Because he was desperately lonely," I suggested.

"Because he had no other economists to disagree with," she laughed and cackled, and cackled and laughed.

It had never occurred to me that some people felt so strongly about economists.

"They're in the pot for a reason," Ma continued, stirring the stew again. "We just don't need them in Pemberland. The way our city works, that's what tells us which way is up."

This made sense to me.

"I think you may be right.".

"Of course, I'm right, you dickhead. And I can provide you with an ironclad, 100 per-cent, definitive proof that I am," she exclaimed, pounding on the floor with the butt of her oar to emphasize the point.

"I'm all ears."

"You and your fucking blue ears. I'm going to have a short nap. Come back in an hour and I'll serve you the proof on a plate."

I obeyed and walked out onto the street and to the nearest washroom to find a mirror and check whether my ears were in fact blue. They were. I thought of a new saying, "Sticks and stones may break my bones, but words will only make my ears turn blue." It didn't bear repeating.

I filled in the extra time doing an errand, and after an hour, I was back at Ma's place.

"Welcome back, young sprout," she said. "I think the stew is ready."

She had laid out two settings on the dining table at the other end of her space, complete with cloth napkins and a basket with pieces of baguette. There was also a bottle of red wine and glasses on the table. The label on the bottle said "Beaune – Clos des Mouches." It looked pretty pricey. I wondered what the occasion was.

Using a ladle, she served me a big plate of stew and one for herself, and we dug in. For a woman on the far side of ninety, and frail as a sparrow, she had a surprisingly lively appetite.

Afterwards, keeping with her French theme, Ma, the Chinese continental cook, produced *crème brulées* and espresso coffee.

I won't say that waiting for the proof she had promised interfered with my enjoyment of the dinner, but it was on my mind, and while finishing my espresso, I prodded her.

"So, Ma, where is this definitive proof of yours?"

She looked at me, beaming.

"You just ate it, motherfucker. And wasn't it delicious?"

She had snookered me again, but the dinner was so good, I didn't mind at all. Something she had said earlier floated into my head, and finally it came to me: "I'll serve you the proof on a plate." Aha!

"And those ground-up economists gave it a certain *je ne sais quoi*," I threw out, saluting her with my empty espresso cup. I had dredged up that bit of French from God knows where. I was beaming, too. It must have been the wine.

14

The Reluctant Lover

Ready-Mix dropped by one evening. She said she had something for us. She and Bark Lady were good friends, so we saw a lot of her.

The "something" turned out to be a couple of theatre tickets.

"You guys have got to come," she said. "The male lead, Twisty Collar, that's a stage name, is a project of mine. Have I ever told you about him?

"No, eh? Well, here's the story. This guy shows up in Dindonkey's office looking for housing, and after Dindonkey is done with him, he sends him to me for a job, the usual thing. He's from Ottawa in the Other World, an oddball. Now think of all the faraway places our refugees come from and how they have to adapt to a new way of life. Twisty was more out of place in Pemberland than any of them.

"Finding him a job was the most difficult assignment I've ever had. He didn't seem to have any real training. He just mumbled something about politics. His résumé was useless, too, even if I could trust it, which I wasn't inclined to do. To make matters worse, he was totally alienated. He had fallen out from his old life, but couldn't put it behind him. He didn't seem to fit into any job, even the most ordinary kind. Of course, I did an optic analysis on him, but it came up dry. That had never happened to me before.

"And then it came to me. I can't explain how. There was something about him, some intangible something, that had escaped even my optic analysis. He was a natural comedian!"

"So you made him a home-care worker," I joked. "Old people like to be entertained."

"Laughter is the best medicine," Bark Lady added.

"Talk about comedians. You two!" Ready-Mix laughed. "No, I found him a place at Backmountain Stage, a small studio group, where he did backstage work and got his foot in the door as a performer. He's never looked back. The Pemberland Arts Company took him on and he's become something of a star. I had him pegged. He's a brilliant comic."

"What's the name of the play?" Bark Lady asked.

"Here it is, on the ticket," Ready-Mix said, handing the two tickets over to us. "The Reluctant Lover. But be forewarned. The other player is Annie Evergreen, and any play she's in is likely to be risqué. And she's a master of the smutty *double entendre*. Come to think of it, maybe Jack shouldn't go. He's so innocent."

I laughed.

"Don't worry about me. Don't you know I have a doctorate in dirty jokes from Rugger University? I even have the certificate."

This last bit was a friendly poke at Ready-Mix for the certificates on her wall.

We showed up on the given date, several weeks later, for the première no less, as Ready-Mix's guests. The cover of the program had the essentials.

THE RELUCTANT LOVER
A Comedy in One Act
A collective production of the PAC's cast and crew
Twisty Collar – Earnest Politician
Annie Evergreen – Ardent Pursuer

"Collective production," Ready-Mix told us, was a bit misleading. Twisty, her protégé, would have provided most of the lines.

The theatre was abuzz with people. The bell went. We took our seats. The curtain rose.

As soon as Twisty appeared on the stage, before he even said a word, the audience laughed. On the surface, it had nothing to do with the way he looked. The audience expected to laugh, Ready-Mix explained to me later, and they were so keyed up that, just by showing his face, Twisty got the laughter started.

He was in a dark blue suit and a tie. He took a few more steps and, grimacing, stuck his finger underneath his collar at the back of his neck, the nervous gesture of the button-down man whose collar was too tight. The laughter increased. There was even some applause. It was, apparently, a signature move which his fans in the audience all recognized. Twisty Collar, get it? He still hadn't said anything.

The plot went something like this. Annie Evergreen, as the Ardent Pursuer, was trying to get Earnest Politician, played by Twisty, into bed and to become pregnant. No matter what she tried though, Earnest Politician misinterpreted what she said and went off on his own tangent. The reluctant lover! It was very clever.

I can't remember everything, but I'll try to recreate the scene for you.

They were on a terrace, with wicker chairs and a glass-topped wicker table. The Ardent Pursuer put all of her sexual charms to work, accidentally on purpose rubbing herself against him whenever she could. Bending over to put their drinks on the table, for example, she brushed her boobs against his arm. He looked at his arm, alarmed, as if something were growing out of it.

Then she went to work on his tie. "I so love your tie," she cooed, "but it needs a little straightening," which straightening she proceeded to do, caressing his chest and slowly moving her hand lower and lower down the tie. You could hear the audience holding its breath.

"I hope it's not wrinkled," he said, looking down at her hand at the bottom of his tie.

"I definitely hope it's not wrinkled," Ardent declared enthusiastically, looking down further.

"TV studio lights show up any wrinkles," Earnest went on, unaffected. "Even outside, the new digital cameras are so good, they can pick up wrinkles at fifty paces."

"So that's why you like wearing hardhats at campaign events," Ardent said, not losing a beat. "Hardhats don't wrinkle. But then the public can't see your sexy hair. Did I ever tell you that your hair turns me on?"

"Do you think women vote for me because of my hair?" Earnest asked excitedly.

"Oh, I don't know about them, but it certainly gets to me in *my* ballot box," Ardent said in her sultry voice.

She had stood up and was now behind him, kissing his ear. With a burst of affection, she mussed up his hair. He bolted upright, knocking her over. She did a backflip. He tried desperately to smooth out his hair.

"Mussed hair sometimes can work," he lectured her, "but there's mussed hair and mussed hair. The muss needs to fit the occasion. I have a special muss I use when I'm promising to defend the middle class. I'm proud of it."

"Wow! A middlemuss!"

"What? No, I call it a 'left muss' when I'm campaigning… ," he demonstrated, "and a 'right muss' after I've got their vote."

"So impressive! Is there a bust muss?"

"Never heard of it. How do you like my suit?"

"I love it. Is it hard to take off?

"It's especially tailored to stay on. If I took it off, I would lose power. Dark blue is a power colour. Brown, on the other hand, is a disaster."

"I know a brown that is even more powerful than dark blue."

"You do?"

"Yes, it's so powerful that if you touch it in the right place, you get an electrical charge, and then you can go on to electrify your audiences. Would you like me to show you how it works?"

"Okay. It sounds interesting."

"You'll have to undo my blouse for just the right brown."

He started to do so, but waking up, suddenly stopped.

"On second thought, I can't... can't... switch to brown. I can't because... because... my staff insists on dark blue! That's it! And if I don't give in to my staff, I'm in trouble."

"But that's what I'm trying to get you to do, give in to your staff!' She stamped her foot. "Should I show you how *that* works?"

The theatre audience was now bubbling with laughter. Remember, too, it wasn't just the lines, it was two first-class comedians doing their schtick – their faces, their timing, their body language – particularly Ardent mimicking and sending up Earnest behind his back and touching him suggestively.

And when Earnest started in on politics proper, the laughter went through the roof.

"Don't you feel like a change of scenery, Earnest?" Ardent asked passionately. She was massaging his neck and rubbing her head against his. "Why don't we just run away, the two of us, all by our lonely selves, and start making babies? A jug of wine, a loaf of bread and thou, beside me on a nice soft bed?"

"Just the two of us?"

"Yes, just the two of us."

"Why would we do that? Two isn't statistically significant. A thousand is better, but not by much. I usually think in hundreds of thousands. We need five hundred thousand extra people in the country."

"Five hundred thousand people is a lot of people for just one bed."

"Do I have to explain everything? We put them to work in our mattress factories. We need them to make mattresses, to solve the mattress shortage. And here's the beauty of it: They can produce enough mattresses so that only 22.5 people on average end up on each mattress."

"Twenty-two point five people?" Ardent exclaimed in disbelief.

"We've worked it out. I mean to say, our consultants, Magoon and Company, have worked it out, and they're the experts. We know they are because we've paid them enough money to make them the experts. If we had paid them less, they wouldn't be the experts we made them, so we would be selling ourselves short."

"Magoo and Company?"

"Magoon and Company, ending in g-o-o-n, goon."

"Isn't that what I said?"

"Let's round it off to twenty-two people per mattress."

"That would make it a promiscuous mattress."

"Did you say 'promiscuous mattress'? That's just brilliant! Promiscuous Mattress! A great name! Even better, it has a nice innovative ring to it! A big new idea! It could become one of the leading international brand names, since everyone in the world needs a mattress. Promiscuous Classic Double. Promiscuous Queen. Promiscuous King. Promiscuous Twin. Promiscuous Memory Foam. The possibilities are endless. We can ride it hard, take credit for it. The 'innovation' thing!"

"You can't get twenty-two people on even a king-size mattress."

"Wrong. It all depends on how the sleepers are arranged. Right now, too many people sleep on the edge of the mattress in order to avoid bumping into others, and some fall off the edge. We need to make better use of the middle. As things stand, we have a missing middle. Deal with the missing middle and the problem solves itself."

"Oh, forget about the damned mattresses!" Ardent shouted. Then, changing her tactics, she sat on his lap, and put a hand inside his jacket. "We don't need a mattress, do we? Not us. We can start making babies right here on the floor, um, and then buy a house, our own house, and live in paradise."

Earnest Politician was trying desperately to get her away from his face so he could speak over her.

"But there's a housing crisis. We also need more new people in the country to build a house for us."

"House, shmouse. And who's going to build a house for those new people if they're busy building a house for us?"

He stood up abruptly, throwing her onto the floor. "That's it!" he cried excitedly. His eyes were shining. "You've asked just the right question! We'll bring in more immigrants to build a house for them, who are building a house for us. Then we'll bring in more immigrants to build a house for *them*, who are building a house for *them*, who are building a house for us. Then we'll bring in more immigrants to build a house for *them,* who are building a house for *them*, who are building a house for *them*, who are building a house for us. Then we'll bring in…"

He was so excited at having uncovered this great idea and how logical it was, he couldn't stop. He had lost it.

Ardent Pursuer, meanwhile, was picking herself up off the floor. She stabbed the air with her fingers and made other rude gestures.

"…to build a house for *them,* who are building a house for *them*, who are building a house for *them*…"

She staggered downstage and spoke directly to the audience. She was wailing.

"What am I going to do? I've tried everything. I'll never get him to stop now. I think he's afraid that if he stops, his world will come to an end. He thinks his palaver is all he's got left to save him. But what about me?"

"…to build a house for *them,* who are building a house for *them*, who are building a house for *them*..," Earnest Politician kept yattering.

"Why don't you take off his clothes?" someone shouted from the audience.

The audience cheered.

Ready-Mix told us afterwards that the cast had planted someone in the audience to come up with the line.

"What a fine idea!" exclaimed Ardent Pursuer. She raised her hands in appreciation. "I'll get on it right away! Oh, it will be just fine!"

"...to build a house for *them,* who are building a house for *them*, who are building a house for *them*..."

She began taking off his jacket, and then his shirt and tie.

"What broad shoulders you have, my dear. And look at all that hair on your chest. It's an enchanted forest."

The curtain began slowly coming down.

"And is this an innie I see before me?"

"To build, them, house, for, house, house, who, build," Earnest Politician worked hard to get the words out, but they were now jumbled.

She had his belt off at this point and was beginning to unzip his trousers, while he looked on in disarray and kept talking, repeating what had become gibberish. The curtain finished its descent.

"Who! For! Yes! House! Building! Oh! Oh! Who!" The Earnest Politician's cries were heard exploding from behind the curtain.

"Whoopee!" came Ardent Pursuer's own shout, this one ecstatic. "Baby, here we come!"

The audience by this time was out of control, some with tears in their eyes from laughing so hard, the laughter still rolling across the room in waves. People were standing up and clapping in unison. It was quite a scene.

I knew, of course, why they were laughing so hard. It wasn't just that Earnest Politician was so indifferent to Ardent Pursuer's desires, and Annie Evergreen was quite a beautiful woman to boot. It was that what he was saying was so goofy, the very stuff of comedy. Pemberlandians had all the housing they needed and more, without their population increasing. In fact, they had no housing problem exactly because their population wasn't increasing. And the more earnest the Earnest Politician was, the funnier the satire.

Except for me. I must have been the only one in all that crowd who wasn't rocking with laughter. I had been watching the Earnest Politician too intently. I was doing optic analysis on him. Okay, I was eyeballing him. He spoke with such seriousness and conviction, I just couldn't laugh.

The curtain was going up again, and there were Annie Evergreen and Twisty Collar taking their bows. Twisty had his pants and shirt back on, although not his jacket. Annie's blouse was rebuttoned. The audience was clapping, laughing, and cheering, some raising a fist in delight.

Twisty fingered the collar at the back of his neck again and winked at us. More laughter and cheers.

He sauntered off into the wings and came back with a bouquet of flowers, which he presented to Annie. More shouts of "bravo" and clapping. Twisty's grin was as wide as the Pacific Ocean. He blew us kisses. He was laughing himself, enjoying the laughter as much as any of us.

And then it hit me, like a two-by-four across the forehead. The seriousness and conviction? It had all been an act.

Twisty Collar is such a great actor!

15

An Outside Expedition and Back Home to Pemberland

The very next week, Bark Lady and I took a group of friends out for dinner. It had been long-planned. We had decided to get married, and the dinner was a way of announcing our engagement. On top of that, I had my own special reason for our getting together – to thank the group for helping me become a Pemberlandian.

There were seven of us at our table in the Emerald Blue Restaurant that night: Ready-Mix, Dindonkey, Yogi Rasputnik (without his special chair), Sir Willgraph, Ma Shen Li-ping and, of course, Bark Lady and myself. They were now all good friends of mine, as well as being long-time friends of Bark Lady's.

I had tried to have the Minister of Finance join us, too, although I would never call him a friend. I also knew he would have been a handful. He had, though, in my early days in Pemberland, explained why my rent was so low, which I appreciated. And shouldn't a couple announcing their engagement be generous? However, no matter how I tried juggling dates, I couldn't find an evening when Yogi Rasputnik and the Minister of Finance were both available. It occurred to me I had never seen them, anywhere, in the same place together.

We ate and drank, gossiped and laughed. The wine flowed, and so did the wisecracks. Although it wasn't our wedding yet, Bark Lady and I were the object of much good-natured ribbing. Dindonkey, with his wicked sense of humour, was especially in good form. You may remember, too, that of all of us, he was the one who still thought we shouldn't abandon the Other World, that we had a duty to try to help them.

He made me an offer that I couldn't refuse – well, I could, but I couldn't. After a glowing tribute to the beauty, charm, and intelligence of Bark Lady, he pronounced that I wouldn't deserve her unless I undertook some heroic feat to demonstrate my love. He proposed that I make my way into the Other World and tell my story to at least one other person. It would also be telling the story of Pemberland. The sly bastard! He put it in such a way that I didn't have a choice, did I? Besides, Jack Lewicki, ex-rugby fullback, was never one to turn down a challenge, crazy as it might be.

So I sucked it up and here I am. Just by coincidence, my nursing school was on its annual break, so I could get away. Thanks to you, I've accomplished my mission. I've only been away for two days, but I can hardly wait to get back. Besides, I have to return in time for my wedding, don't I?

It was late afternoon, now, heading into evening.

"Let me buy you dinner, too," Jack said, realizing how late it was.

"Not on your life," I replied. "Dinner is on me. What's the point of being a partner in McIntyre, McIntyre, Dhaliwal, and Rosen if not to make a lot of money and be able to treat my friends?"

I called the server over and asked him to give us a Latin dinner assortment, whatever he chose. My head was too full of what I had just learned to bother with a menu. I called my wife again and explained once more the situation.

We ate quietly and afterwards made small talk. I offered him a bed at my place, which he accepted. I then, tentatively, raised a question which I knew I would have to ask but, although I'm a lawyer, wasn't sure how to tackle: Was there any chance of going back to Pemberland with him for a visit?

Jack was skeptical about my chances.

"Listen," I said. "I'm not going to stay and push your numbers over 100,000. There's no way I would leave my family and life here in Vancouver behind."

"I understand," he said, "and would like to help, but that's not how entering Pemberland happens."

"Well, how does it work, then?"

"That's just it, I'm not sure how it works. It seems to be unpredictable. I've only just got in once myself and I still haven't figured it out."

We agreed on a plan. The two of us would go camping at exactly that old spot and reconnoiter the mountainside to see if we could find a crevice that looked like a possibility. We'd use a tent of mine and I'd bring along food for two or three days. I made arrangements with my firm and, of course, with my wife, including an arrangement to pick up my car if I wasn't back in a few days. The next morning, early, we were off.

It took the better part of the day to get there, first in the car and then on foot, with me lugging my pack. We pitched camp and scouted around, but saw nothing. I cooked up dinner on my nifty Swedish Trangia camp stove and we hit the sack.

Lying there, on the inflatable sleeping pads I had brought with us, we shared some old memories, mostly rugby stuff. Suddenly, just by luck, I remembered a question I had meant to ask the day before at the Havana.

"Did you ever figure out that secret measure of prosperity, hidden in those letters revealed to you by the yogi?"

"You mean G D P P C A P P P?" Jack responded, singing the letters out just as he had done the day before. "Actually, I learned the answer sooner than I expected. Are you ready?"

"Uh huh."

"Gross domestic product per capita at purchasing power parity," Jack pronounced with a grandiose flourish. "It's a mouthful," he chuckled. "The key to understanding it is the two words 'per capita' – what it comes down to for each person. I have a confession to make. I've become a bit of an economist. Jack Lewicki, concrete truck driver and soon-to-be nurse, a do-it-yourself economist. Would you believe it? I come out at night and haunt honest people. Just don't tell Ma Shen about it."

On that, we fell asleep.

I slept particularly well. When I finally woke up, Jack wasn't in the tent. I stuck my head out, but he wasn't outside, either. After strapping on my boots, I circled around a fair distance, but there was no hide nor hair of him. I guess I wasn't surprised.

Later that morning, opening my toilet kit, I found a couple of ticket stubs.

> *THE RELUCT…*
> *A Comedy in…*
> *Pemberland A…*

Followed by fragments of date and time. Jack had left them behind for me. I still have them.

I hung around for a couple more days until my food ran out, but nothing came of it, which also didn't surprise me, and I headed home. I mulled over our meeting and soon realized what I had to do – write out his account and get it down on the record. It was my share of an unspoken bargain. I've done my best. I might not have gotten every detail right, and some of the language might be mine rather than Jack's – and I threw in a lot for continuity – but I'd say I've done a fairly good job.

I've come to the sad realization that I'm not going to get to Pemberland in my lifetime, and after that, what is there? I think of Jack and his friends often. I'll never forget them.

Acknowledgements

Bryce Leigh, with the Whistler section of the Alpine Club of Canada, generously shared his mountain knowledge with me, whereupon I settled on the Cayoosh Range and located the crevice through which Jack ended up discovering Pemberland. The city was there all the time, I realized. Rob Riecken also helped with details about hiking in the mountains. Marian Cook, Brett Dehay-Turner and William Rees took the time to carefully read my penultimate draft and provided me with invaluable feedback and suggestions. Their perspicacity and attention to detail were impressive. Finally, my wife, Marguerite, not only served as editor-in-chief, recommending some changes and bringing the usual author's lapses to my attention, but also did the copy editing and advised on umpteen other matters. They all, together, have my gratitude for helping to get Jack's story across.

About the Author

HERSCHEL HARDIN is an author, playwright, commentator, and former radio broadcaster, newspaper columnist, magazine writer, economic historian, lecturer, community organizer, public-interest advocate, quixotic political candidate, consultant, and corporate director. He has also been deeply involved in charity work. As he explains it, if you live long enough, you end up willy-nilly doing at least a few things. He lives in West Vancouver, B.C., with his wife, Marguerite.